Contents

Getting Started

If you have bought this book, you will already know that scoubidouing is a great way to have fun!

Scoubidou projects can be as simple or as complicated as you choose. This book gives instructions on how to do the basic stitches as well as some of the more complicated ones. There are also a variety of projects that use these techniques and give you further tips on how to make your scoubidous even more exciting.

So, get scoubidouing – you can do it!

Basic Materials

There are many different makes of scoubidou strands; some strands are sparkly and see-through, others are in solid colours. Try the solid colours if you want a smoother-looking finish to your projects and the sparkly ones if you want to jazz them up.

Val Mitchell and Selina Collins

CASSELL

First published in the United Kingdom by Cassell & Co.
The Orion Publishing Group
5 Upper St Martin's Lane
London WC2H9EA

Authors: Val Mitchell and Selina Collins
Photography: Val Mitchell and Selina Collins
Design, typesetting and illustration: Steve Hawes

Produced for the Orion Publishing Group by SMPS Ltd, Kedington, Suffolk

A CIP record for this book is available from the British Library

ISBN 0304368164

Printed in Italy

A Few Extras

Adding extra decorations to your projects makes them special. Many toy shops sell coloured beads, and junk shops are an excellent place to find old necklaces that you can break up to create interesting tassels. Thin wire has a variety of uses: picture wire can be good to make your projects bend (available in most DIY shops); jewellery wire (available from craft shops) comes in different thicknesses – the thinnest are useful for sewing on beads and other extras. Slightly thicker wire can be used to thread through two or more strands to create larger projects.

Personalising everyday objects is not only fun, but useful too. Adding a scoubidou project to a luggage tag can make suitcases easy to find at airports; key-rings and belt hooks are simple to decorate and can be bought from key cutting shops quite cheaply.

… and don't leave the pets out! Why not attach a scoubidou to your dog's lead or one of your cat's toys? Scoubidouing can be fun for the whole family.

'Off We Go' Stitches

These stitches show you how to begin your projects. If you want to create a bigger loop to attach your final project to, wrap one of your first loops around a pencil like this. Look at the **'Moving On'** section to see the types of designs you can create, beginning with these **'Off We Go'** stitches.

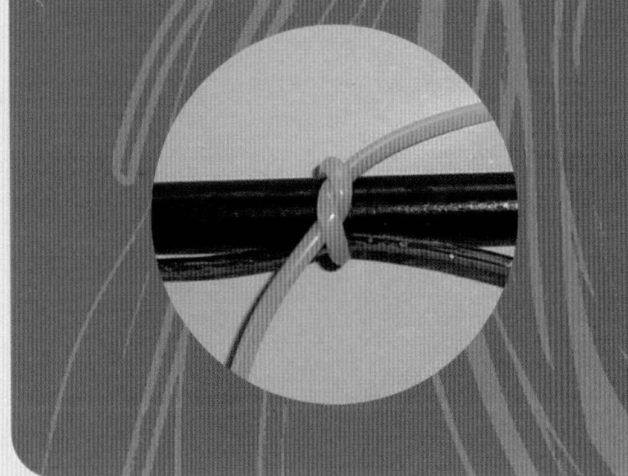

'Off We Go' Box Stitch

This stitch can be used to start projects using **'Moving On' Box Stitch** and **'Moving On' Round & Round Stitch**.

a Find the mid-point of each strand and lay strand 3–4 across strand 1–2.

b Bring strand 1 up and loop it over strand 3–4, between strands 2 and 4. Bring strand 2 up and loop it over strand 3–4, between strands 1 and 3.

c Take strand 4 over the loop next to it and under the second loop, into a position between strands 2 and 3 in this diagram.

d Now work in the opposite direction. Take strand 3 over the loop next to it and under the second loop. This should end up in a position between strands 1 and 4 in the diagram.

e Pull the strands together slowly.

f To tighten the stitch up, it is easiest to pull all the strings with equal strength. The final stitch will look a bit like a chessboard pattern.

g The other side of the stitch looks like this.

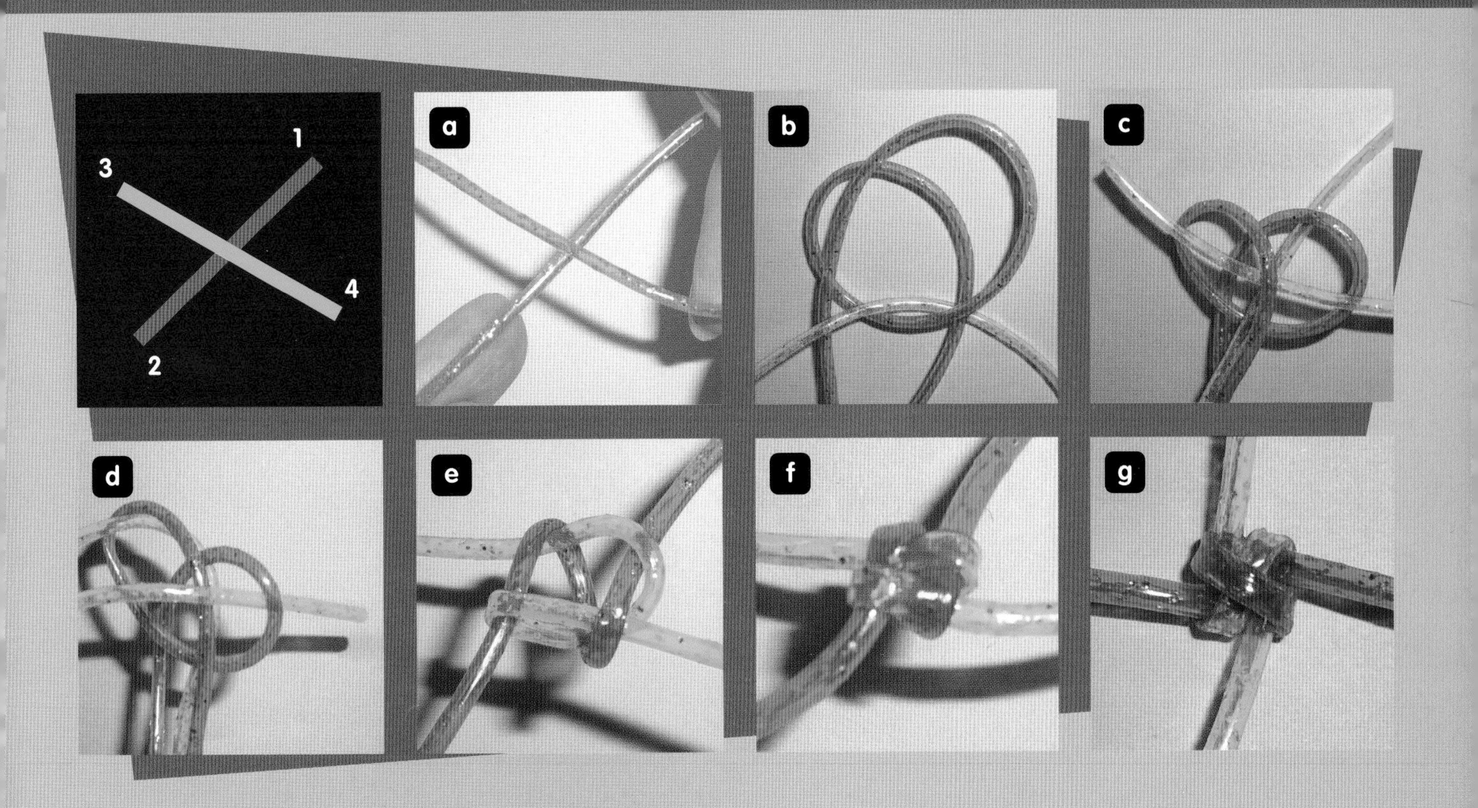
3
1
4
2
a
b
c
d
e
f
g

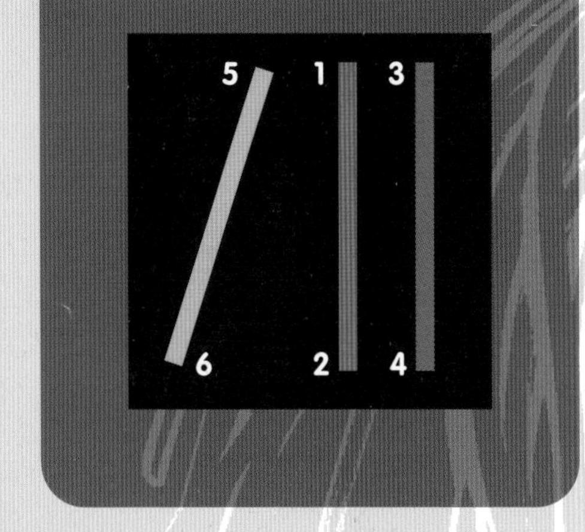

'Off We Go' Wrap It! Stitch

This stitch can be used to start projects using **'Moving On' Wrap It! Stitch**.

a Take two strands of equal length and make sure the ends match up together. Tie a granny knot like this.

b Thread strand 5–6 through one loop of the granny knot.

c Pull it through so that the middle of the strand makes a loop around the knot strand.

Pull the knot tight.

d Take strand 4 over strands 5 and 6, then under strand 2.

e Take strand 2 under strands 5 and 6, then out through the loop made by strand 4.

f Pull the knot tight like this.

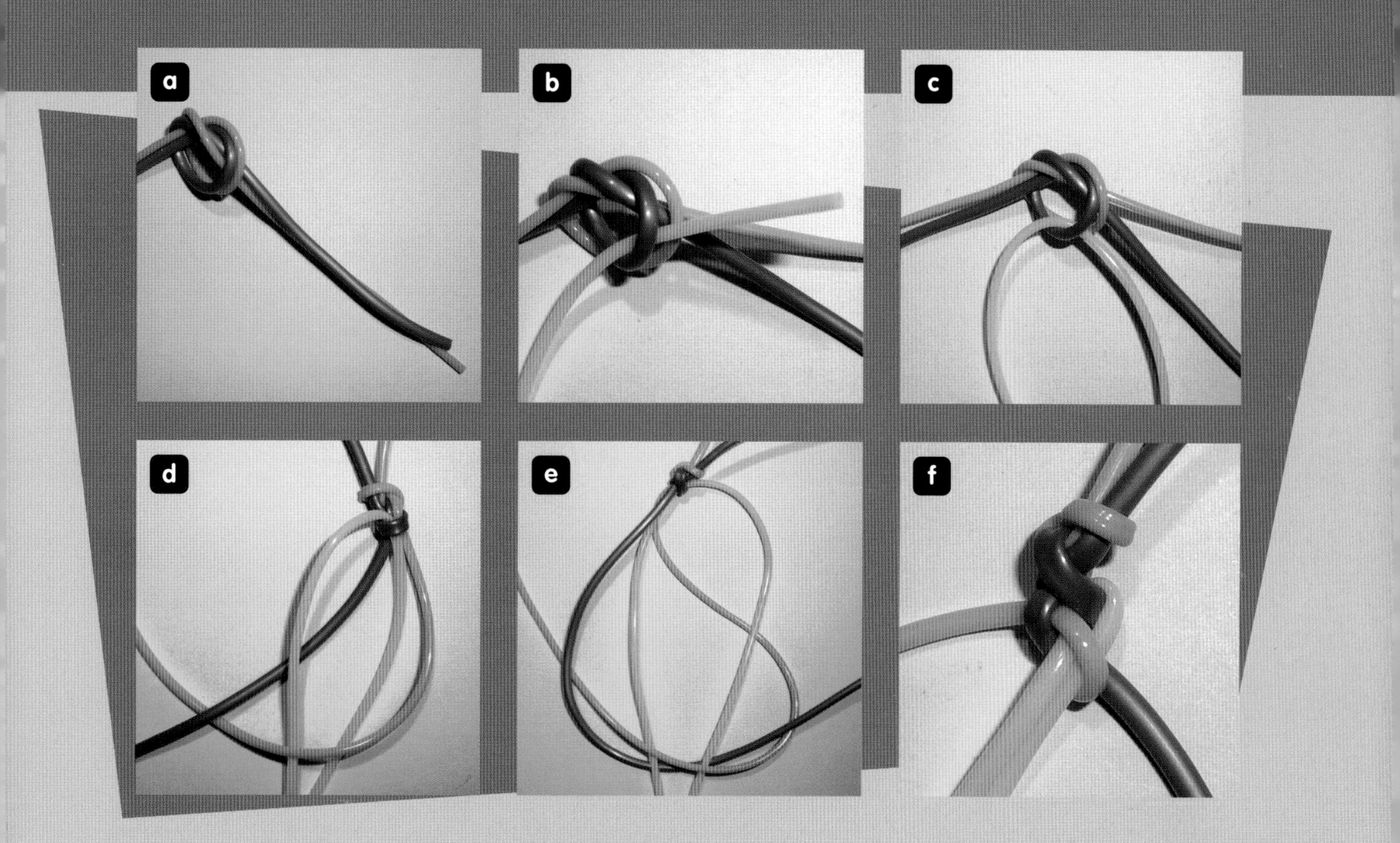
a
b
c
d
e
f

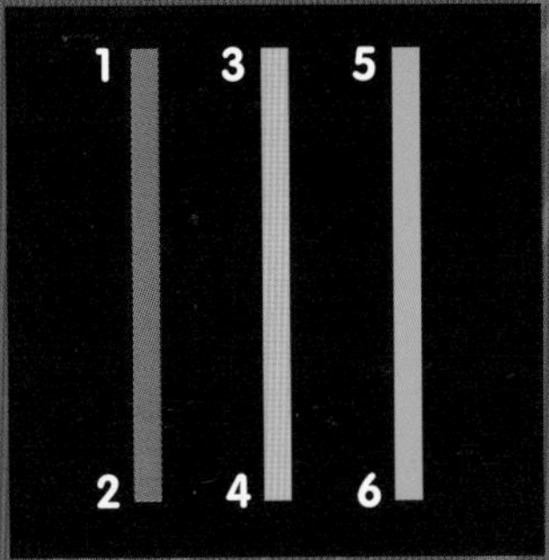

1 3 5

2 4 6

'Off We Go' 1, 2, 3 Stitch

This stitch can be used to start projects using **'Moving On' 1, 2, 3 Stitch**.

a Tie a granny knot in all three strings to secure ends 1, 3 and 5.

b Separate out the long strands (2, 4 and 6).

c Take strand 2 over strand 4 and hold to make a loop.

d Now pass strand 4 over strand 6 and hold to make a second loop.

e Take strand 6 and pass it through the loop you made with strand 2.

f Pull the strands slowly with the same strength in opposite directions to make the stitch.

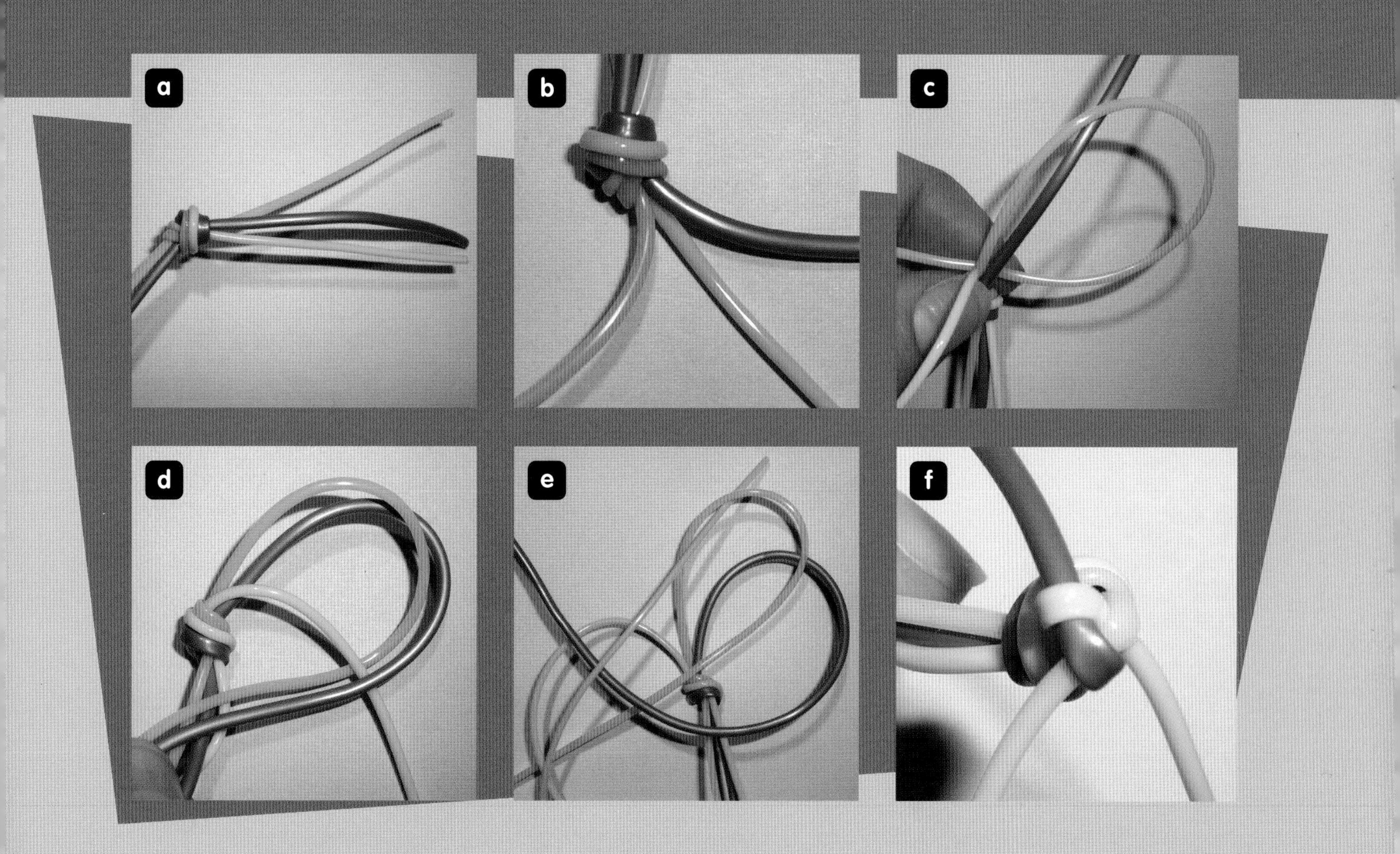
a
b
c
d
e
f

'Off We Go' Over & Under Stitch

This stitch can be used to start projects using **'Moving On' Over & Under Stitch** and **'Moving On' Do the Twist! Stitch**.

a Lay strands 1–2 and 3–4 over strand 5–6.

b Pass strand 5 over the centre strands, and make a loop between strands 3 and 6. Then pass strand 6 over the centre strands and make a loop between strands 5 and 2.

c Take strand 1 (working left to right) over the loop next to it and under the second loop. Take strand 2 (working right to left) over the loop next to it and under the second loop.

d Take strand 4 (working right to left) over the loop next to it and under the second loop.

e Take strand 3 (working left to right) over the loop next to it and under the second loop.

f Pull the strands slowly, with the same strength, in opposite directions to make the stitch.

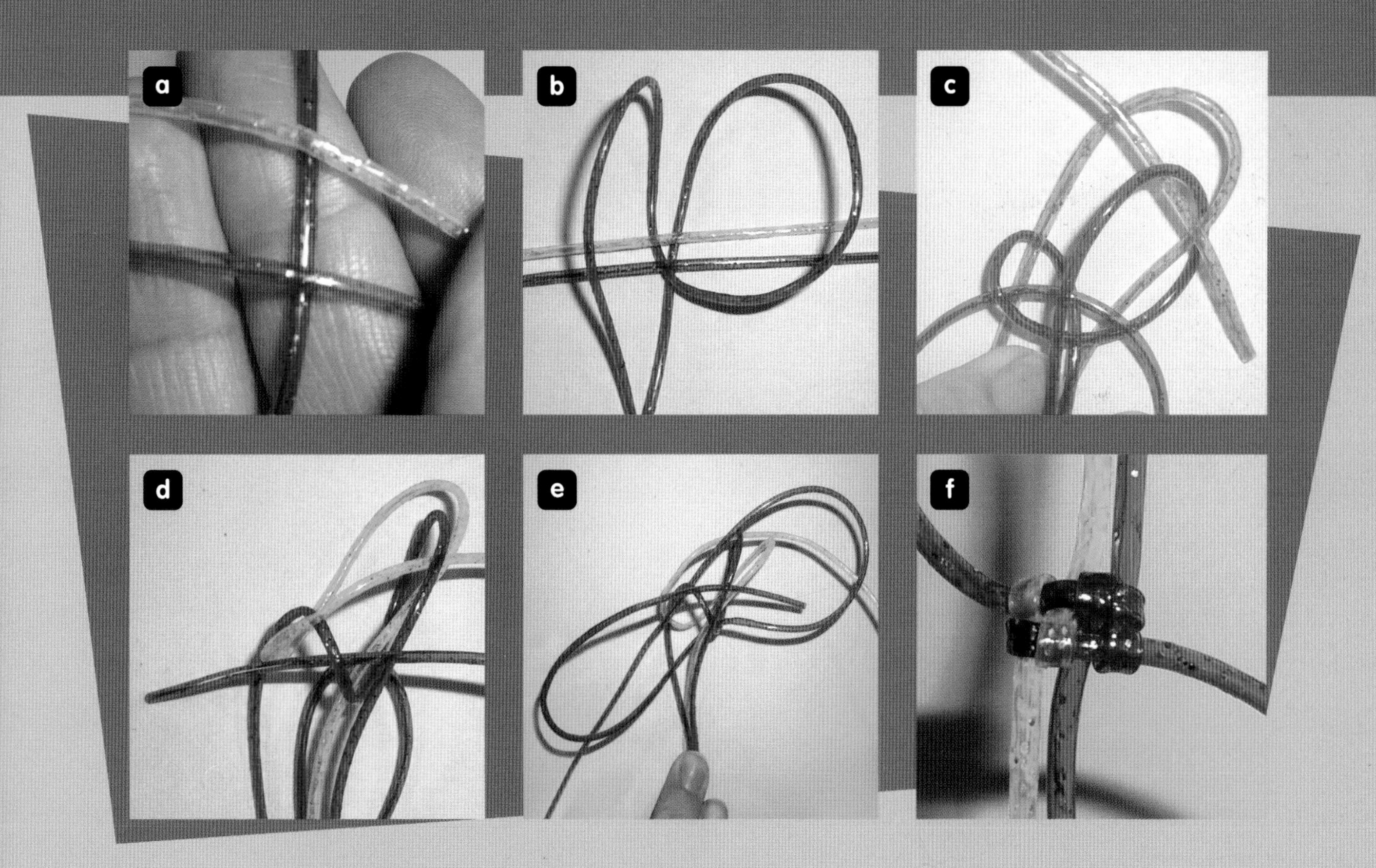
a
b
c
d
e
f

'Moving On' Stitches

These stitches show you how to create the main part of your project. Try changing stitches like **'Moving On' Box Stitch** and **'Moving On' Round & Round Stitch** part way through a project to see what happens!

'Moving On' Box Stitch

This stitch is good for creating fairies and lizards.

a Begin with an **'Off We Go' Box Stitch** as shown here (see pages 6–7).

b Bring strand 1 (black in the picture on the right) up and make a loop with it between strands 2 and 4. Bring strand 2 (the second black strand) up and make a loop with it between strands 1 and 3.

c Take strand 4 (the yellow strand nearest to you), working right to left, over the loop next to it and under the second loop.

d Now work in the opposite direction. Take strand 3 (the yellow strand furthest from you) over the loop next to it and under the second loop.

e Pull the strands together slowly and tighten the stitch up.

f For the next stitch, the direction reverses (see diagram above).

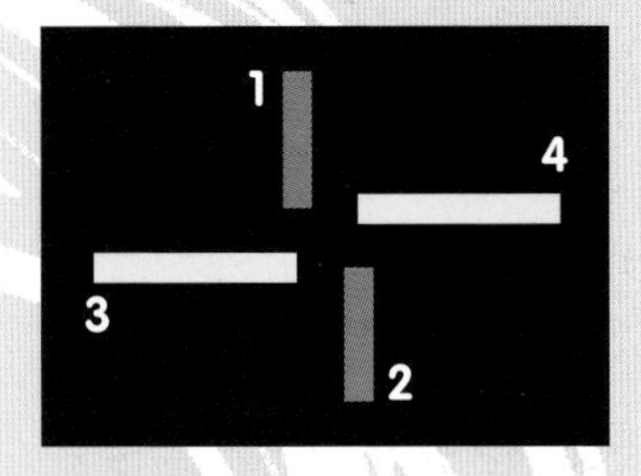

Make a loop with strand 1 between strands 2 and 3; make a loop with strand 2 between strands 1 and 4.

Now, working right to left, pass strand 4 over the first loop and under the second. Finally, take strand 3 (working left to right) over the first loop and under the second.

g Keep alternating the stitches in this way until your project is complete.

Turn to page 36 to see how to finish off a **Box Stitch** project.

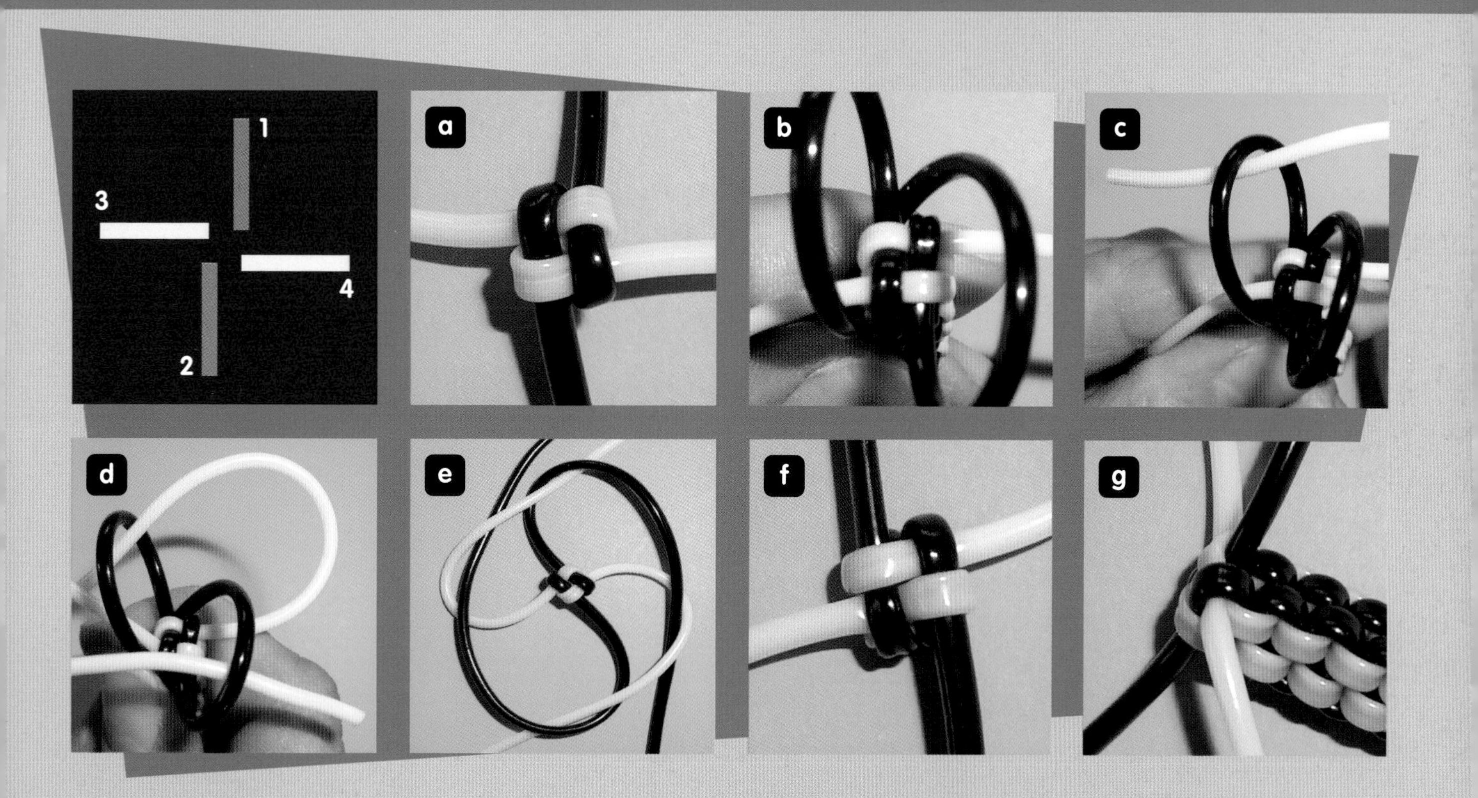
1
3
4
2
a
b
c
d
e
f
g

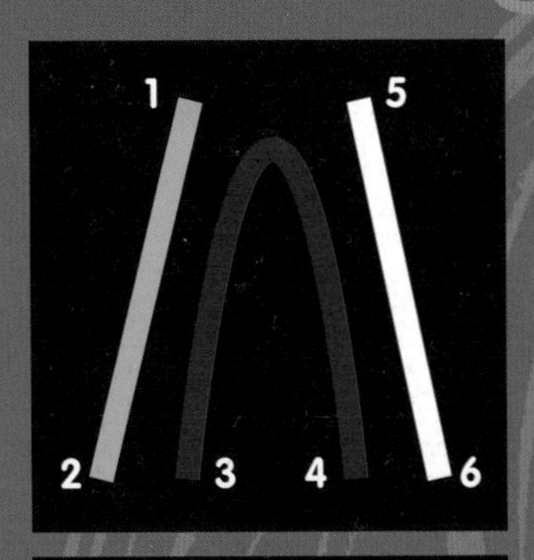

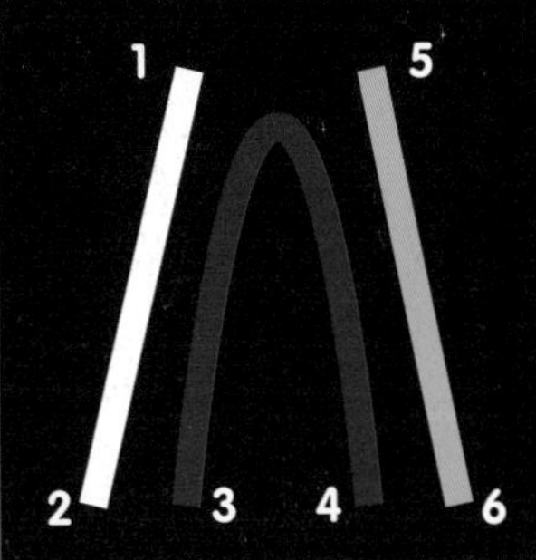

'Moving On' Wrap It! Stitch

This stitch is good for creating bracelets and snakes.

a Begin with an **'Off We Go' Wrap It! Stitch** as shown here (see pages 8–9).

Take strand 2 (the blue strand in the picture) across the front of strands 3 and 4.

b Bring strand 6 (white in this picture) over the top of strand 2, passing it under strands 3 and 4, before …

c … finally threading it through the loop made by strand 2.

d For the next stitch, the direction reverses (diagram left, below).

Take strand 6 (the blue strand in the picture on the right) across the front of strands 3 and 4.

e Bring strand 2 (white) over the top of strand 6, passing it under strands 3 and 4, before finally threading it through the loop made by strand 6.

f Keep alternating the stitches in this way until your project is complete.

Finish off your project with some fancy knots (see page 36).

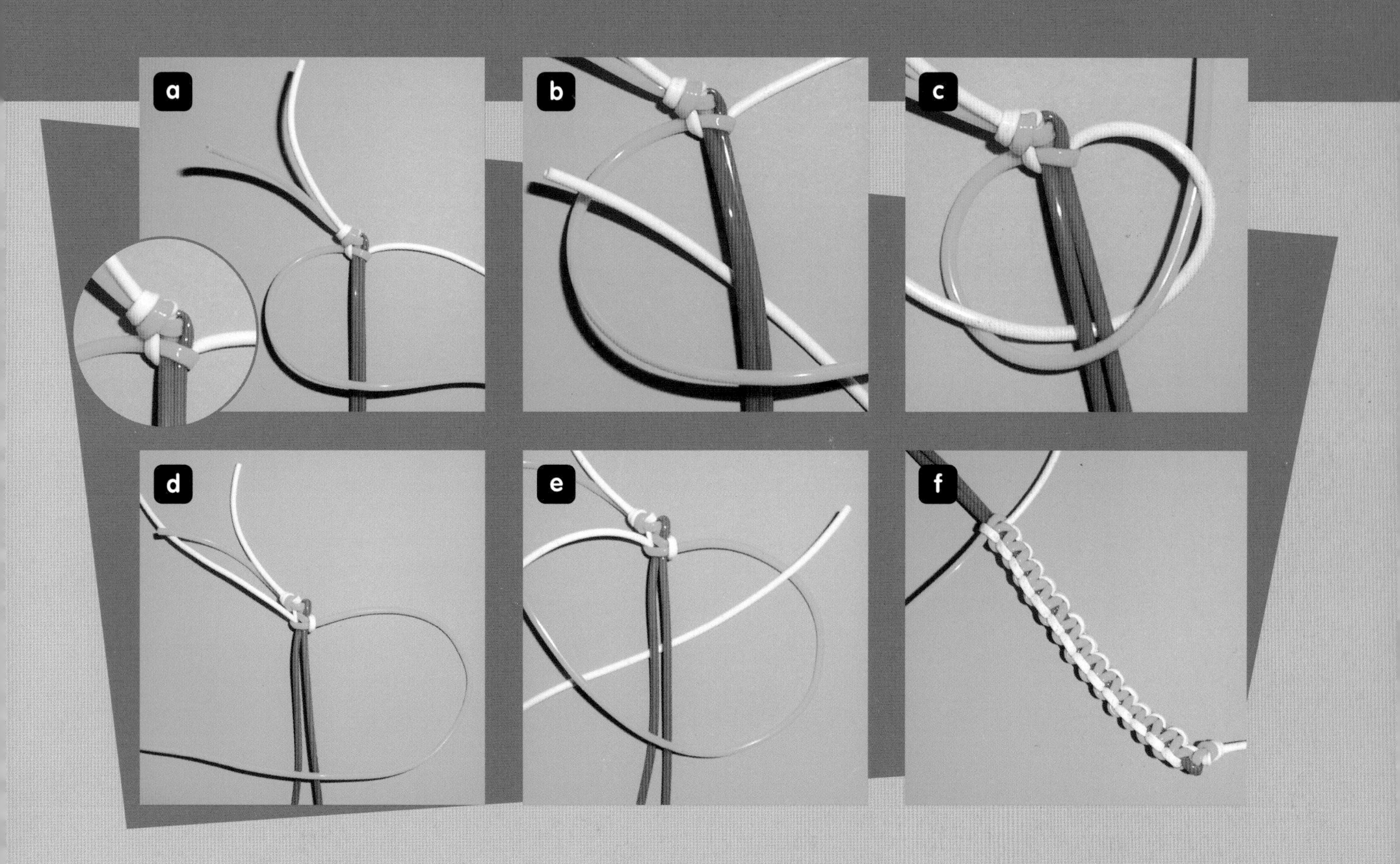
a
b
c
d
e
f

'Moving On' 1, 2, 3 Stitch

This stitch is good for creating tags and key-rings.

a Begin with an **'Off We Go' 1, 2, 3 Stitch** (see pages 10–11).

Take strand 1 (black in this picture) over strand 2 (turquoise in this picture).

b Now take strand 2 around strand 1 (see picture) and over strand 3.

c Pass strand 3 around strand 2 (in the same way as you did with strand 2 in step b) and through the loop made by strand 1.

d Pull the stitch tight.

e Turn the project around so that the coloured strands are all in the position they started at and repeat until your project is finished.

Turn to page 38 to see how to finish off a **1, 2, 3 Stitch** project.

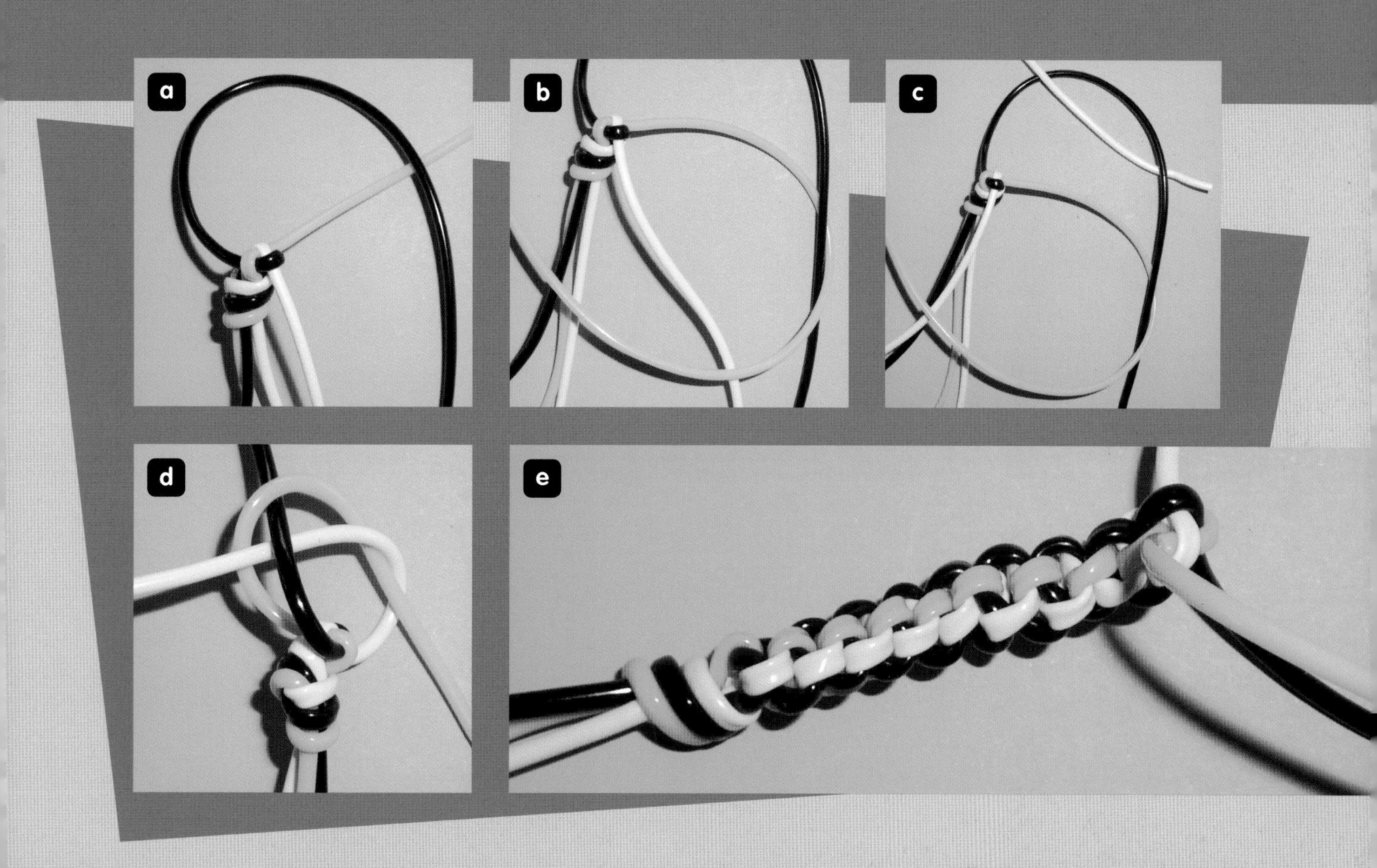
a
b
c
d
e

'Moving On' Helter Skelter Stitch

This stitch is good for creating sea creatures and scrunchies.

You will need four strands to do this stitch.

a Begin this stitch with a granny knot (see right).

b Pass strand 4 over the other three strands …

c … then behind them and up through the loop you have just made.

d Pull the strands tight and continue with the stitch until you have completed your project.

e Now untie the granny knot you made at the beginning and follow the instructions for **Wrap It! Stitch** (see page 16).

f Turn to page 36 to finish your project off with **Box Stitch**.

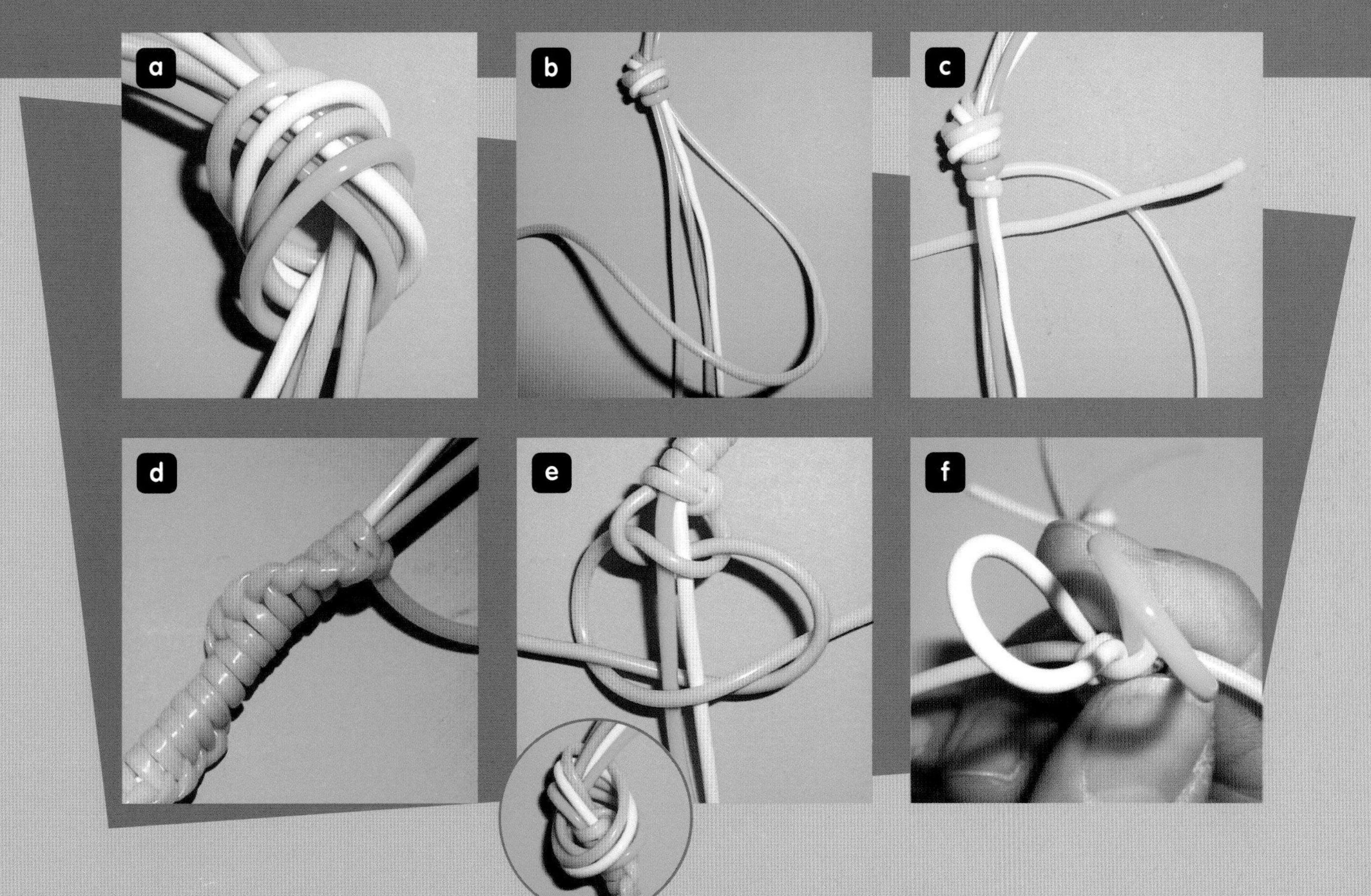
a
b
c
d
e
f

'Moving On' Over & Under Stitch

This stitch is good for creating shrimps and chunky luggage tags.

a Begin with an **'Off We Go' Over & Under Stitch** as shown here (see pages 12–13).

Begin with the black strands (1 and 2 in this picture). Loop strand 1 over strands 4 and 6 to end up between strands 2 and 6. Loop strand 2 over strands 3 and 5 to end up between strands 1 and 3.

b Now take strand 3 (pink in this case), working from left to right, over the first loop and under the second.

Working right to left, take the same colour strand (4) over the first loop and under the second.

c You are now going to work with the final colour. Working from left to right, take strand 5 over the first loop and under the second loop.

d Finally, working from right to left, take strand 6 over the first loop and under the second loop.

e Pull the strands together slowly to make the stitch.

f For the next stitch, the direction reverses (see diagram opposite, right). Begin with the black strands again (1 and 2 in this picture). Loop strand 1 over strands 3 and 5 to end up between strands 2 and 5. Loop strand 2 over strands 4 and 6 to end up between strands 1 and 4.

g Now take strand 4 (pink in this case), working from right to left, over the first loop and under the second. Working with the remaining same colour strand (3), thread this left to right over the first loop and under the second.

h Now for the final colour. Working from right to left, take strand 6 over the first loop and under the second loop. Then, working from left to right, take strand 5 over the first loop and under the second loop, pulling the strands tightly to make the stitch.

Turn to page 38 to see how to finish off an **Over & Under Stitch** project.

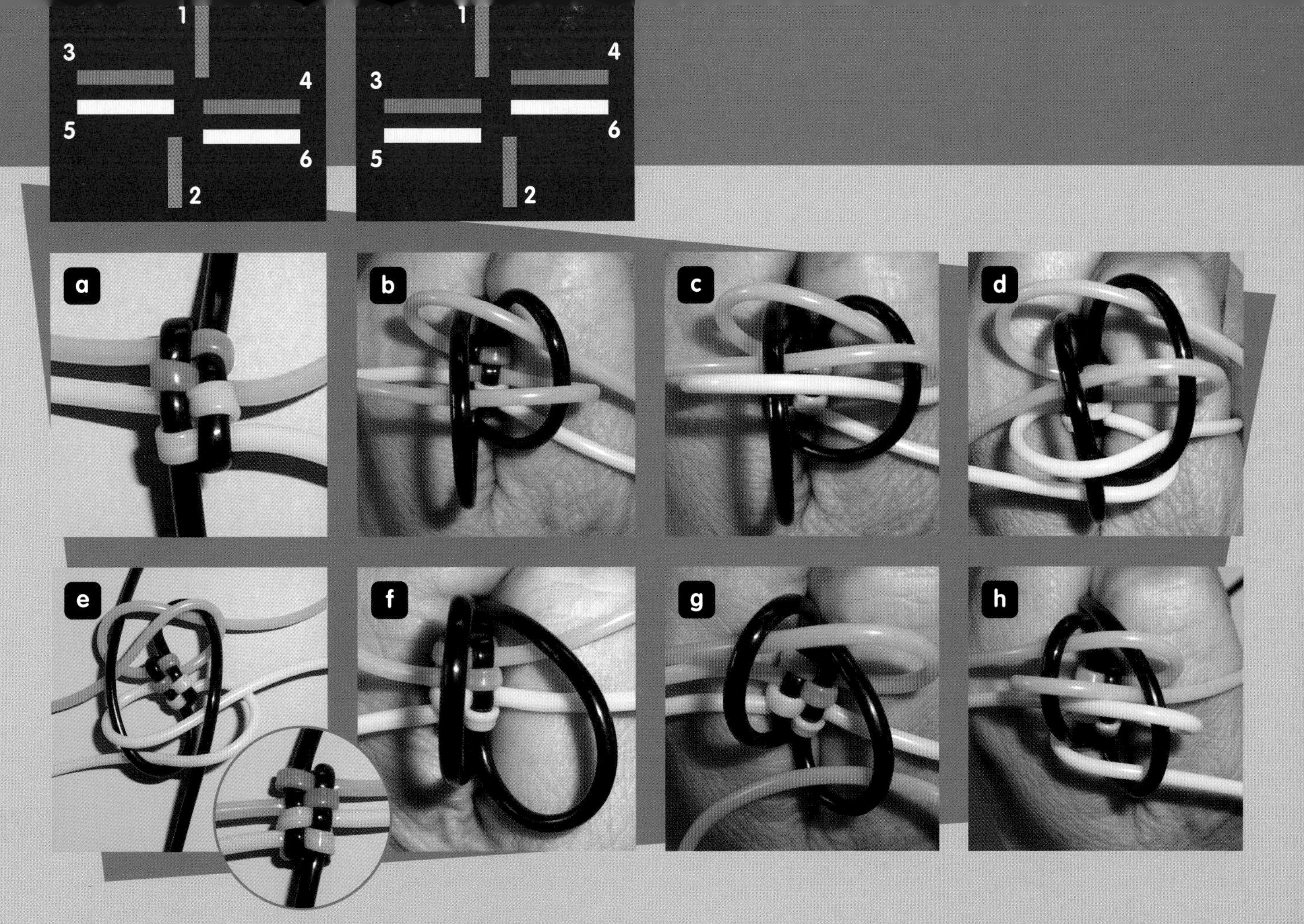
1
3
4
5
6
2
1
4
3
6
5
2
a
b
c
d
e
f
g
h

1

3

4

2

'Moving On' Round & Round Stitch

This stitch is good for creating bracelets and broomsticks.

a Begin this stitch with an **'Off We Go' Box Stitch** (see pages 6–7).

Pass strand 1 diagonally across the checker pattern and between strands 2 and 4 to form a loop.

b Pass strand 2 diagonally across the checker pattern and between strands 1 and 3 to form a second loop.

c Pass strand 3 (working from left to right) over the first loop and under the second loop.

d Pass strand 4 (working from right to left) over the first loop and under the second loop.

e Pull the stitch tight and …

f … continue with your project until it is completed.

Turn to page 36 to see how to finish off a **Round & Round Stitch** project with **Box Stitch**.

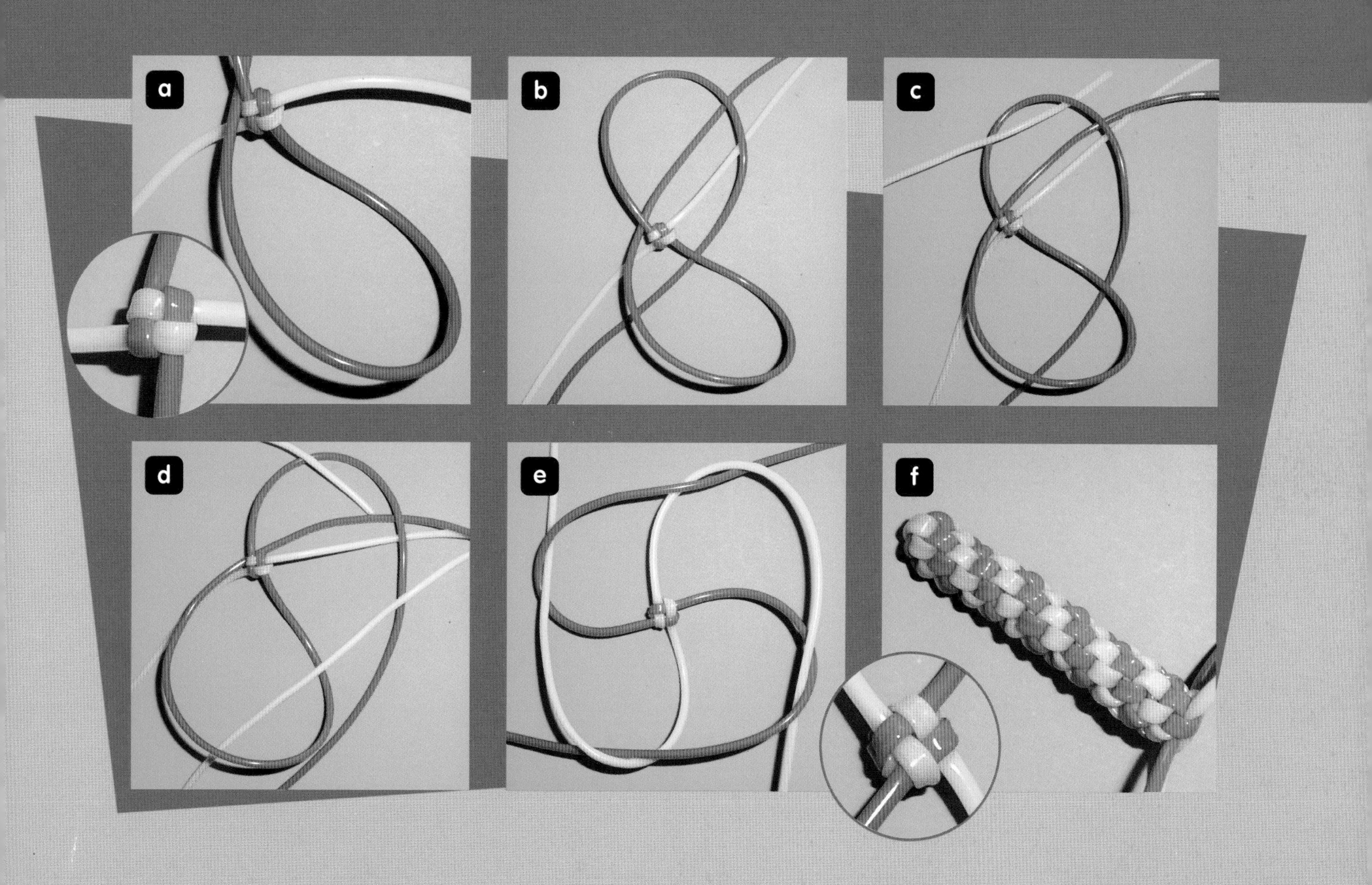
a
b
c
d
e
f

'Moving On' Do the Twist! Stitch

This stitch is good for creating octopuses and shrimps.

a Begin this stitch with an **'Off We Go' Over & Under Stitch** (see pages 12–13).

Pass strand 1 over strand 5 to make a loop between strands 5 and 2.

b Pass strand 2 (the second white strand here) over to make a loop between strands 1 and 3.

c Now strand 3 creates a loop by passing between strands 2 and 4.

d The final strand (strand 4) passes between strands 3 and 6 to make a fourth loop.

e You can now begin to thread. Take strand 6 and thread it over the first loop, under the second loop. Continue to thread over the third loop and under the fourth.

f Now, working from left to right, do the same with strand 5: thread it over the first loop and under the second; over the third loop and under the fourth.

➤ Continued on page 28

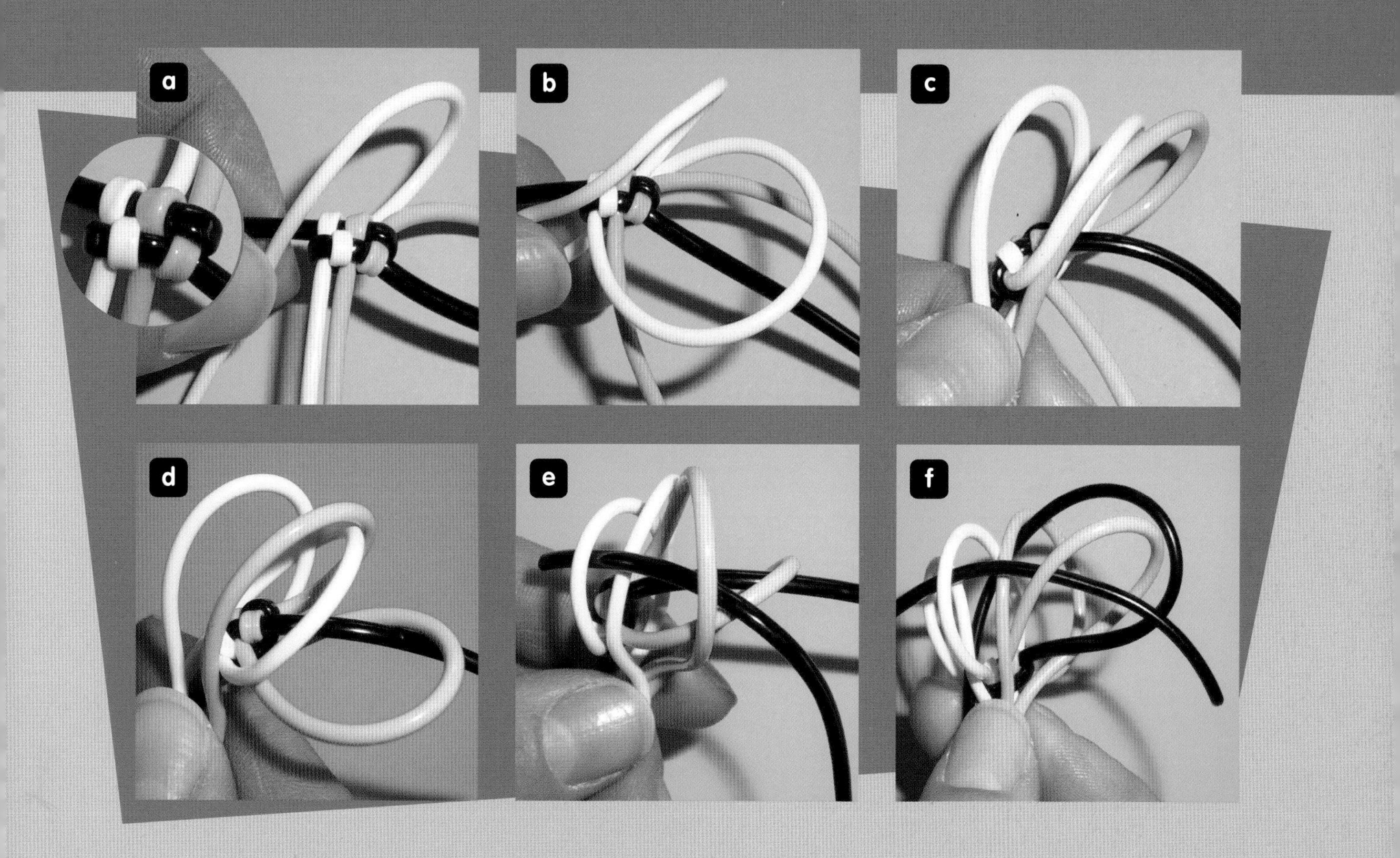
a
b
c
d
e
f

'Moving On' Stitches

➤ **'Moving On' Do the Twist! Stitch** continued from page 26

g Pull the stitch together slowly, taking strands 1, 3 and 6 in one hand; 5, 2 and 4 in the other.

h Begin the next stitch exactly as for the first and continue until you have completed your project.

Follow the instructions on page 38 to finish your project with the **Over & Under Stitch** method.

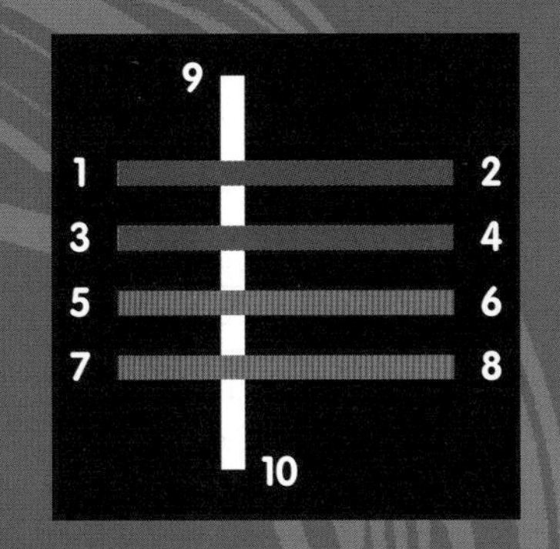

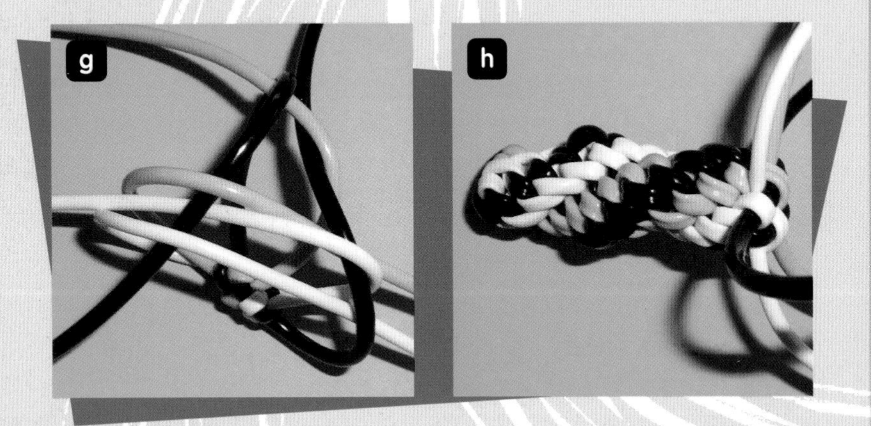

'Moving On' Caterpillar Stitch

This stitch is good for creating large bugs and bracelets.

You will need five strands to do this stitch.

a Find the mid-point of strand 9–10 and secure with a granny knot about 6cm down from strand ends 1, 3, 5 and 7.

b Place strands 9 and 10 down the centre, splaying out strands 2 and 6 on one side, strands 4 and 8 on the other side.

c Loop strand 6 over strands 9 and 10 and under strand 8.

d Loop strand 8 under strands 9 and 10 and up through the loop created by strand 6.

➤ Continued on page 30

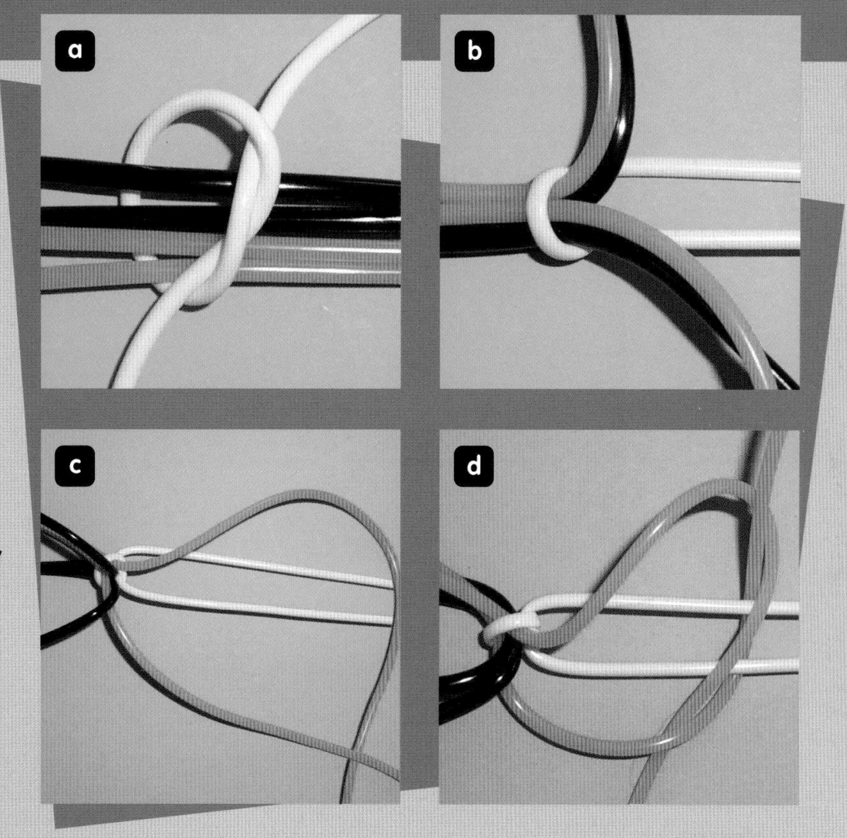

'Moving On' Stitches

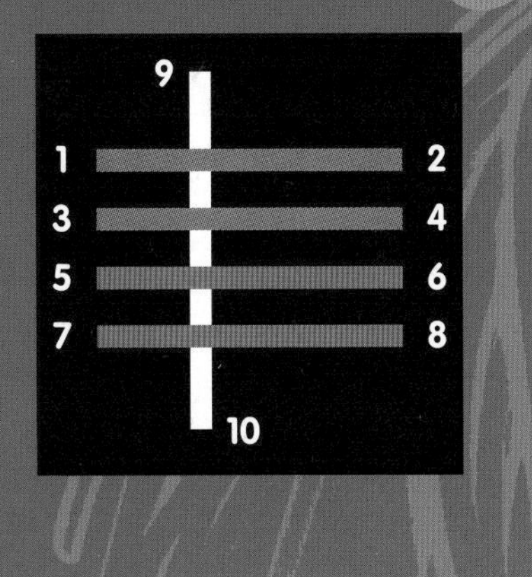

➤ **'Moving On' Caterpillar Stitch** continued from page 29

e Tighten this part of the stitch before continuing.

f You are now going to do the stitch in reverse. Strand 8 is now furthest away from you. Strand 6 is nearest to you (both are pink in these photographs).

Loop strand 6 over strands 9 and 10 and under strand 8. Loop strand 8 under strands 9 and 10 and up through the loop created by strand 6.

g Tighten this stitch.

h You are now going to work with strands 2 and 4 (the black strands in these photographs.

Bring both strands underneath strands 6 and 8 before starting the stitch.

i Create the same two stitches, as shown in stages c–g, but using strands 2 and 4.

j Now go back to strands 6 and 8 and repeat the process. Continue completing two stitches with first one colour and then the other, as shown in the photo, until your project is complete.

Follow the instructions on page 38 to finish your project with the **1, 2, 3 Stitch** method (see the diagram in the left-hand column).

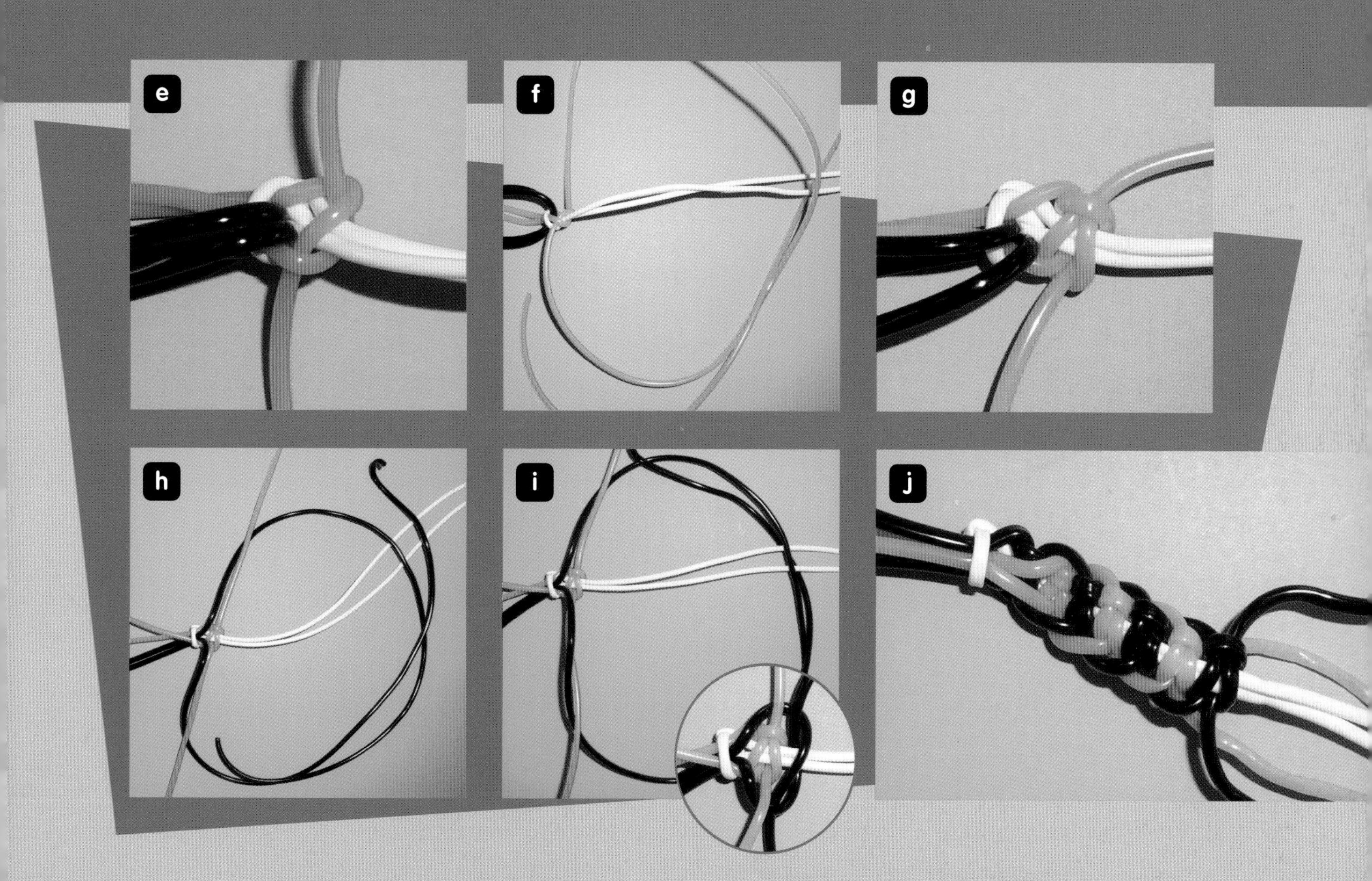
e
f
g
h
i
j

'Moving On' ... and Joining Up

Sometimes you may need more than one length of scoubidou to make the bigger projects, or you may wish to change direction!

There are two main methods for joining the strands and these are illustrated here.

Staggered joins

This join works well for **'Moving On'**: **Box Stitch**; **1, 2, 3 Stitch**; **Over & Under Stitch**; **Round & Round Stitch** and **Do the Twist! Stitch**.

a Make sure the ends of your scoubidou strands are trimmed to different lengths so that you do not make a join more than every three stitches.

Thread in a new strand from the opposite direction and parallel to the strand you are finishing off, like this.

Continue with the next stitch, using the strand you are finishing off.

Pull this very tightly to secure the new strand.

b You can now begin to work with the new strand. Cut the old strand close to the project after you have completed two more stitches.

Wired joins

This join works well for **'Moving On'**: **Wrap It! Stitch**; **Helter Skelter Stitch** and **Caterpillar Stitch**.

It is important to join the strands for these stitches before you begin, otherwise the strands will pull apart.

c Thread a length of jewellery wire through both strands you are intending to join, leaving about 8cm poking out of each end.

When you come close to the join, you will need to hold the wire at the free end of the second strand, so that as you go over the gap, the two strands are pushed together.

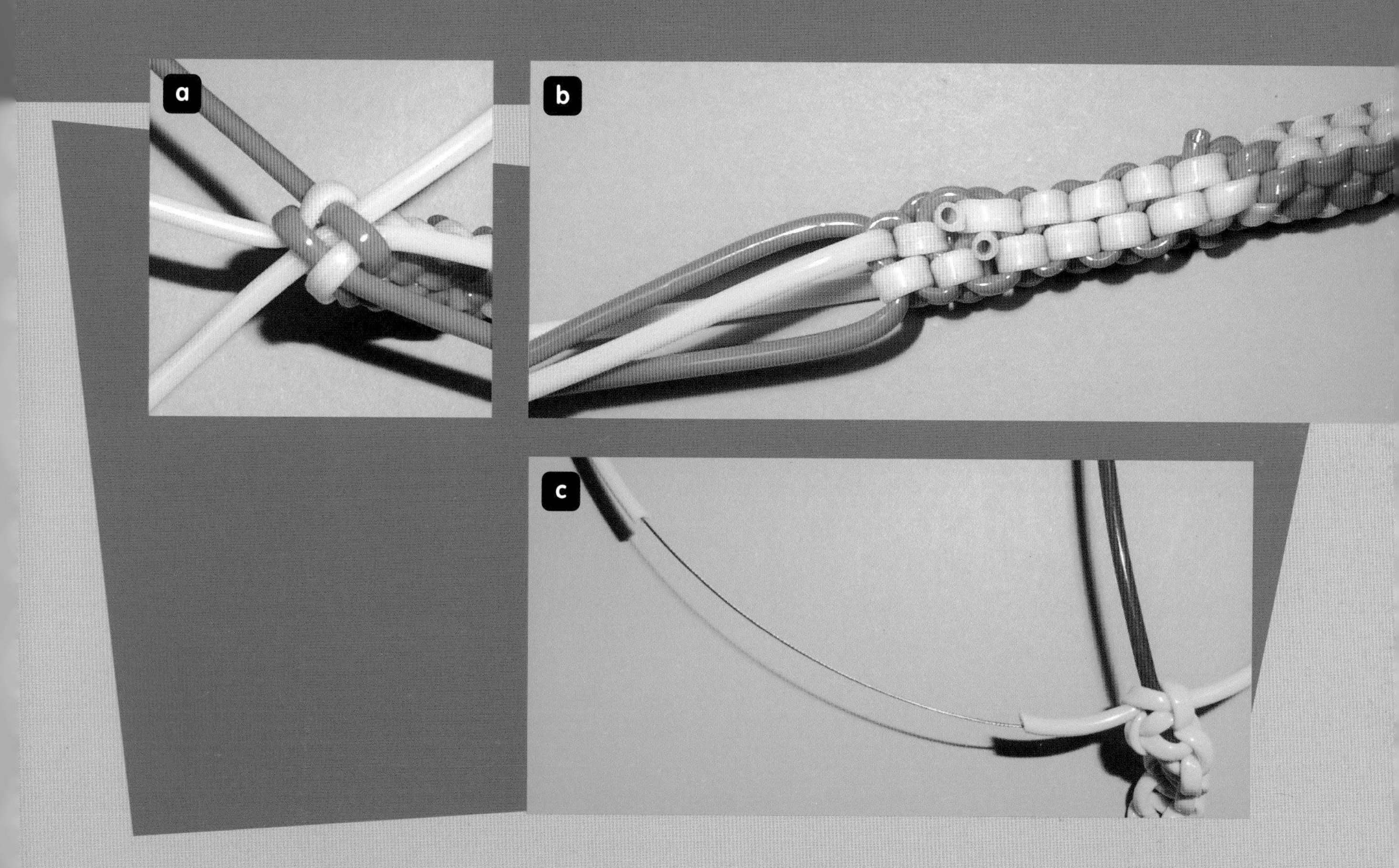
a
b
c

'Moving On' ... and Joining Up

Right-angle joins

These joins can be done with **'Moving On'**: **Box Stitch**; **Over & Under Stitch**; **Round & Round Stitch** and **Do the Twist! Stitch**.

Double join

Try using the double join to add legs to animals.

a Create your two sections to the required length.

Put the two working ends of the project together, you will now begin to work sideways.

Using two (or three for **Over & Under Stitch** and **Do the Twist! Stitch**) strands from each side, continue to create stitches like this.

b Follow exactly the same process on the opposite side of the project ...

c ... and you will then have a neat square hole in the middle.

Triple join

Try using the triple join to make starfish.

d Create your three sections to the required length.

Put the three working ends of the project together; you will now begin to create a six-pointed scoubidou.

Using two (or three for **Over & Under Stitch** and **Do the Twist! Stitch**) strands from each project, continue to create the same stitch ...

e ... until you have six equal lengths. (The diagram on the page opposite shows how the strands work for **Box Stitch**: strands 3 and 4 join to strands 5 and 6; strands 7 and 8 join to strands 9 and 10; strands 11 and 12 join to strands 1 and 2.)

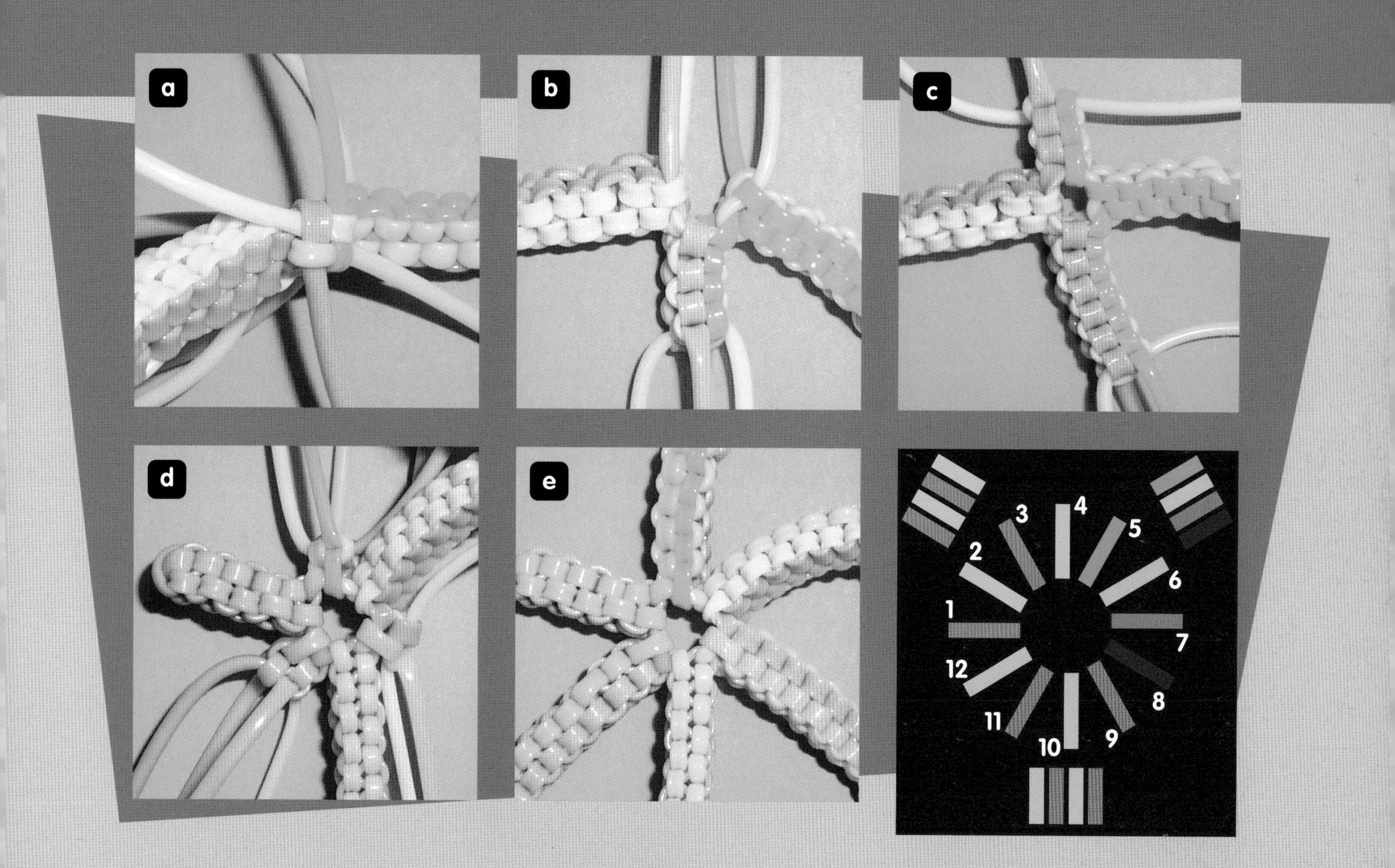
a
b
c
d
e
1
2
3
4
5
6
7
8
9
10
11
12

'Time to Stop' Stitches

There are a number of ways to finish off your scoubidou projects.

Knots are the simplest, and these can be made more interesting if you create a pattern with them, like this.

'Time to Stop' Box Stitch

Take your **Box Stitch** or **Round & Round Stitch** project and...

a Create a **'Moving On' Box Stitch**, leaving it loose like this.

b Take strand 2 under strand 4 and up through the middle of the **Box Stitch**.

c Now take strand 4 under strand 1 and up through the middle of the **Box Stitch**.

d Keep working anti-clockwise. Take strand 1 under strand 3, passing this up through the middle of the **Box Stitch**.

e Finally, pass strand 3 under the loop created by strand 2 in step b, and up through the middle of the **Box Stitch** so that all four strands are pointing in the same direction.

f Pull the strands evenly and tightly to created a rounded end, like this.

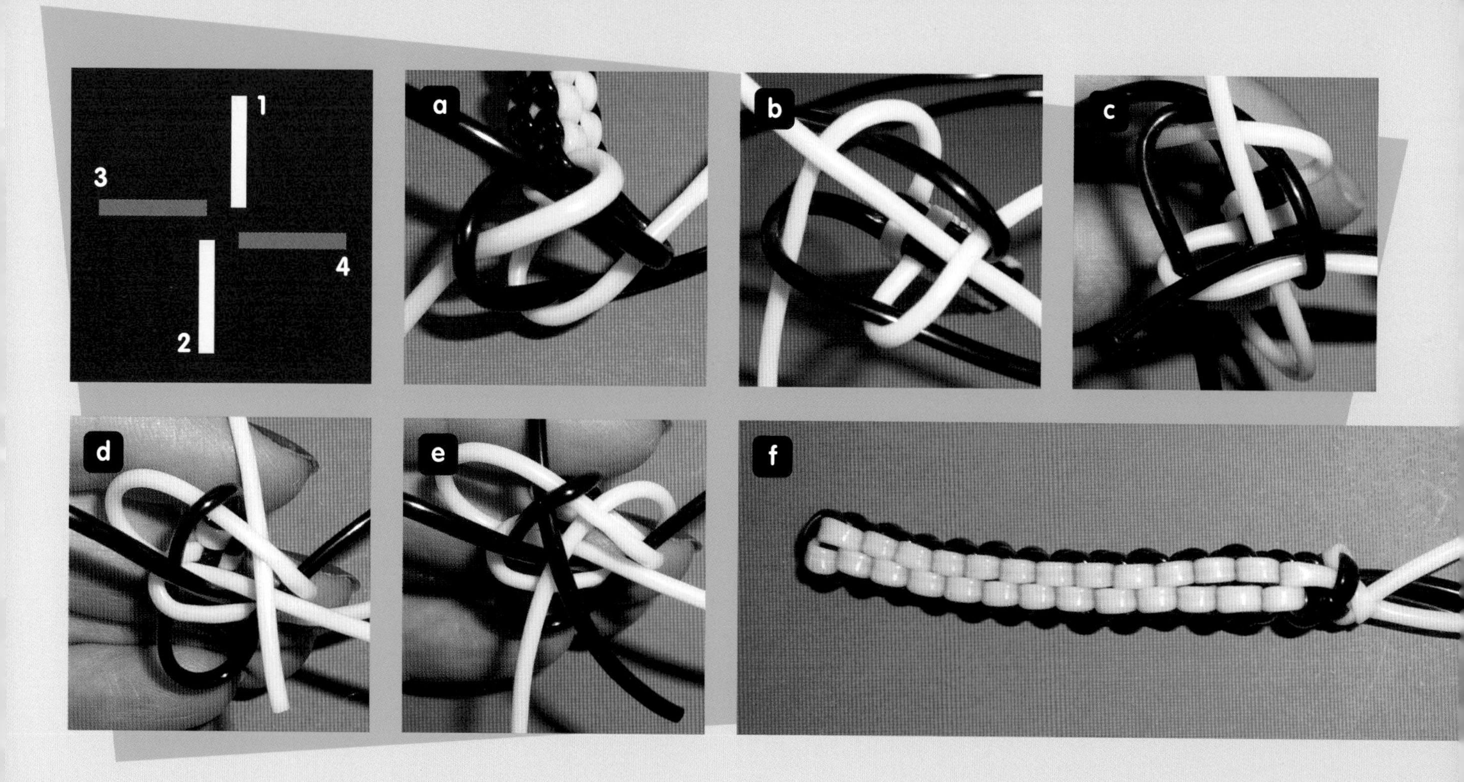
1
3
4
2
a
b
c
d
e
f

'Time to Stop' 1, 2, 3 Stitch

Take your **1, 2, 3 Stitch** project and…

a Create a **'Moving On' 1, 2, 3 Stitch**, leaving it loose like this.

b Working anti-clockwise as you did for the **Box Stitch**, take strand 1 under strand 3 and up through the middle of the **1, 2, 3 Stitch**.

c Take strand 3 under strand 2 and up through the middle of the **1, 2, 3 Stitch**.

d Finally, take strand 2 under the loop created by strand 1 in step b, and up through the middle of the **1, 2, 3 Stitch** so that all three strands are pointing in the same direction.

e Pull the strands evenly and tightly …

f … to create a rounded end, like this.

'Time to Stop' Over & Under Stitch

Take your **Over & Under Stitch** or **Do the Twist! Stitch** project and…

g Create a **'Moving On' Over & Under Stitch**, leaving it loose like this.

h Take strand 1 under strand 3 and up through the upper hole (made by strands 3 and 4) in the middle of the **Over & Under Stitch**.

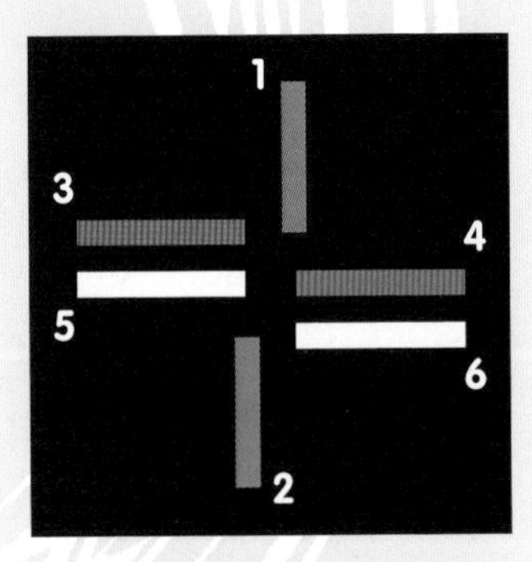

➤ Continued on page 40

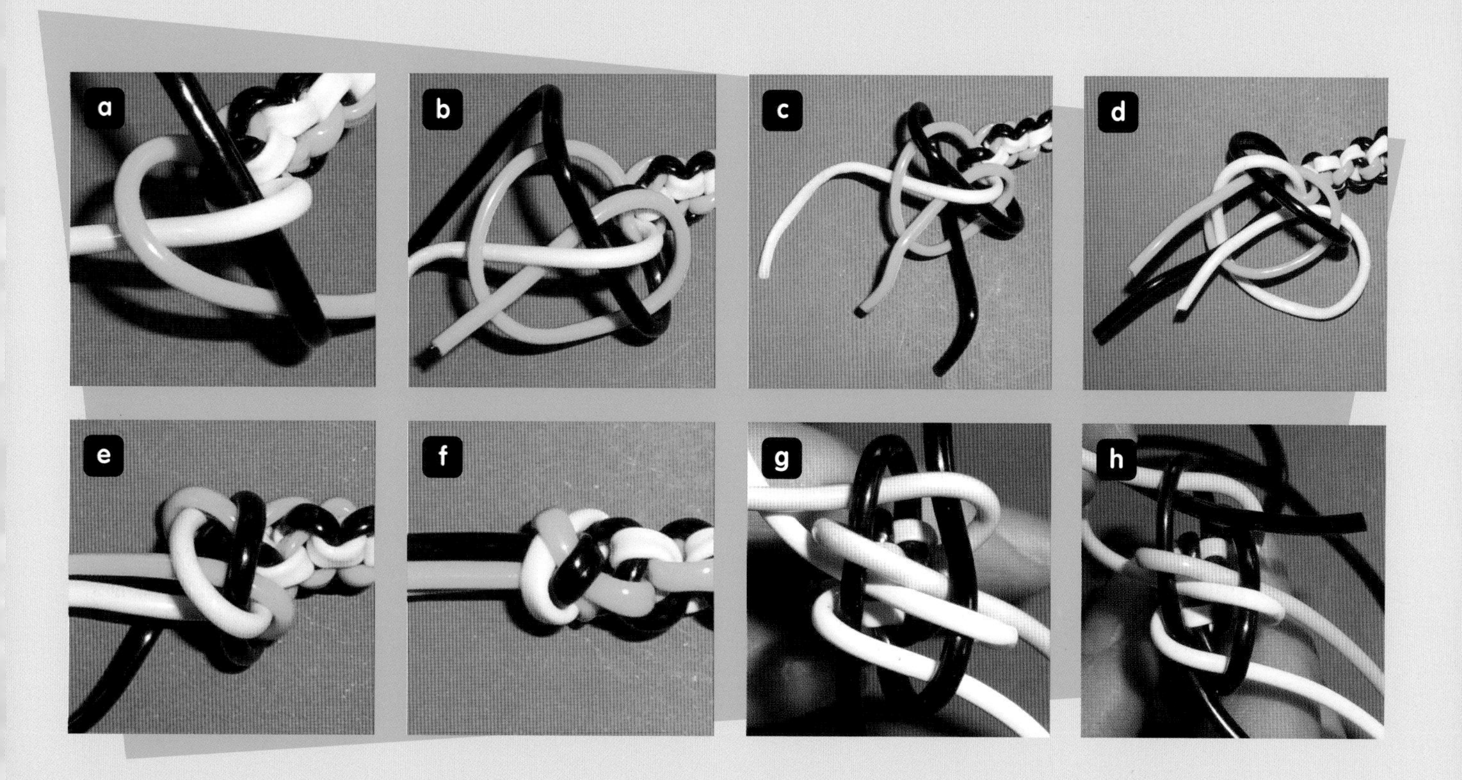
a
b
c
d
e
f
g
h

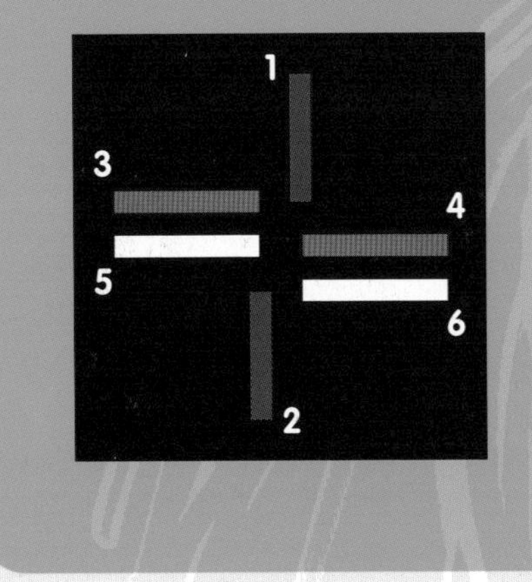

➤ **'Time to Stop' Over & Under Stitch** continued

i Now take strand 3 under strand 5 and up through the lower hole (made by strands 5 and 6) in the middle of the **Over & Under Stitch**.

j Keep working anti-clockwise. Take strand 5 under strand 2, passing this up through the middle of the lower hole.

k Take strand 2 under strand 6, passing this strand up through the middle of the lower hole. You now have three strands through the middle of the lower hole and one through the upper hole.

Now pass strand 6 under strand 4 and up through the middle of the upper hole.

l Finally, pass strand 4 under the loop created under strand 1 and up through the middle of the upper hole. There are now three strands coming through each of the two holes.

m Pull the strands evenly and tightly to created a rounded end, like this.

i

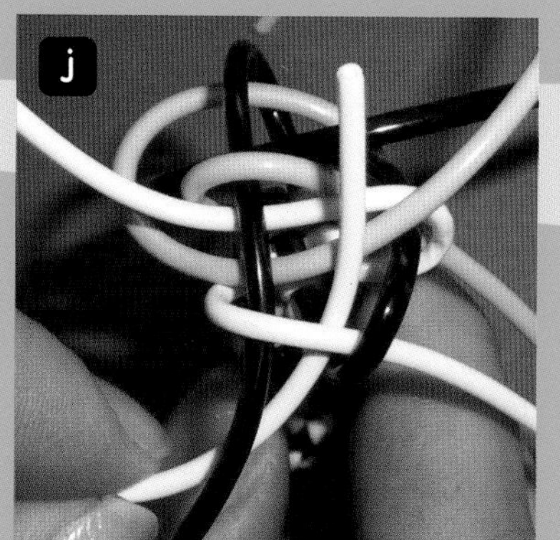
j

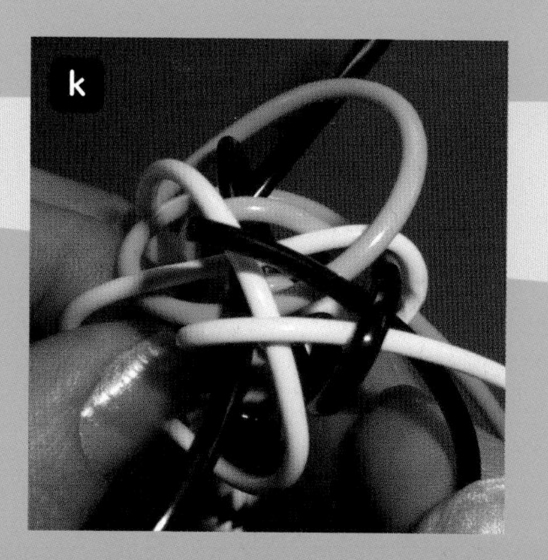
k

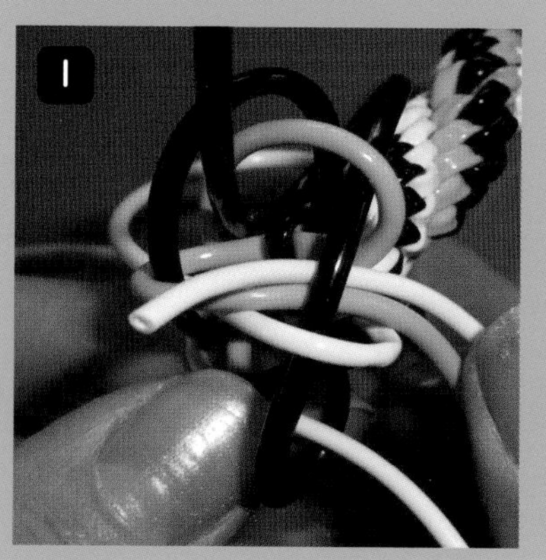
l

m

Tassels and Beads

You can personalise your projects in many ways, and a well finished-off project looks really professional.

Tassels

Think about how to cut the ends of your tassels.

a These free ends don't all have to be the same length and sometimes look more interesting when cut at an angle.

Cutting the ends of the tassels several times creates a fringe effect that can look good for hair!

Beads

Finishing off tassels with beads makes them really individual.

b **Large beads** work well on key-rings. The beads make them heavier and easier to find in a big bag!

c **Small beads** can be used to weave into your projects …

d … to create effects like this.

e These smaller beads can be used as caterpillar tracks, tyres or just to make bracelets and headbands more interesting.

f Try threading a few beads onto a strand, finishing off with a bead to create antennae for insects.

You will see beads used many different ways in the **Let's do It!** section of this book to give you even more ideas.

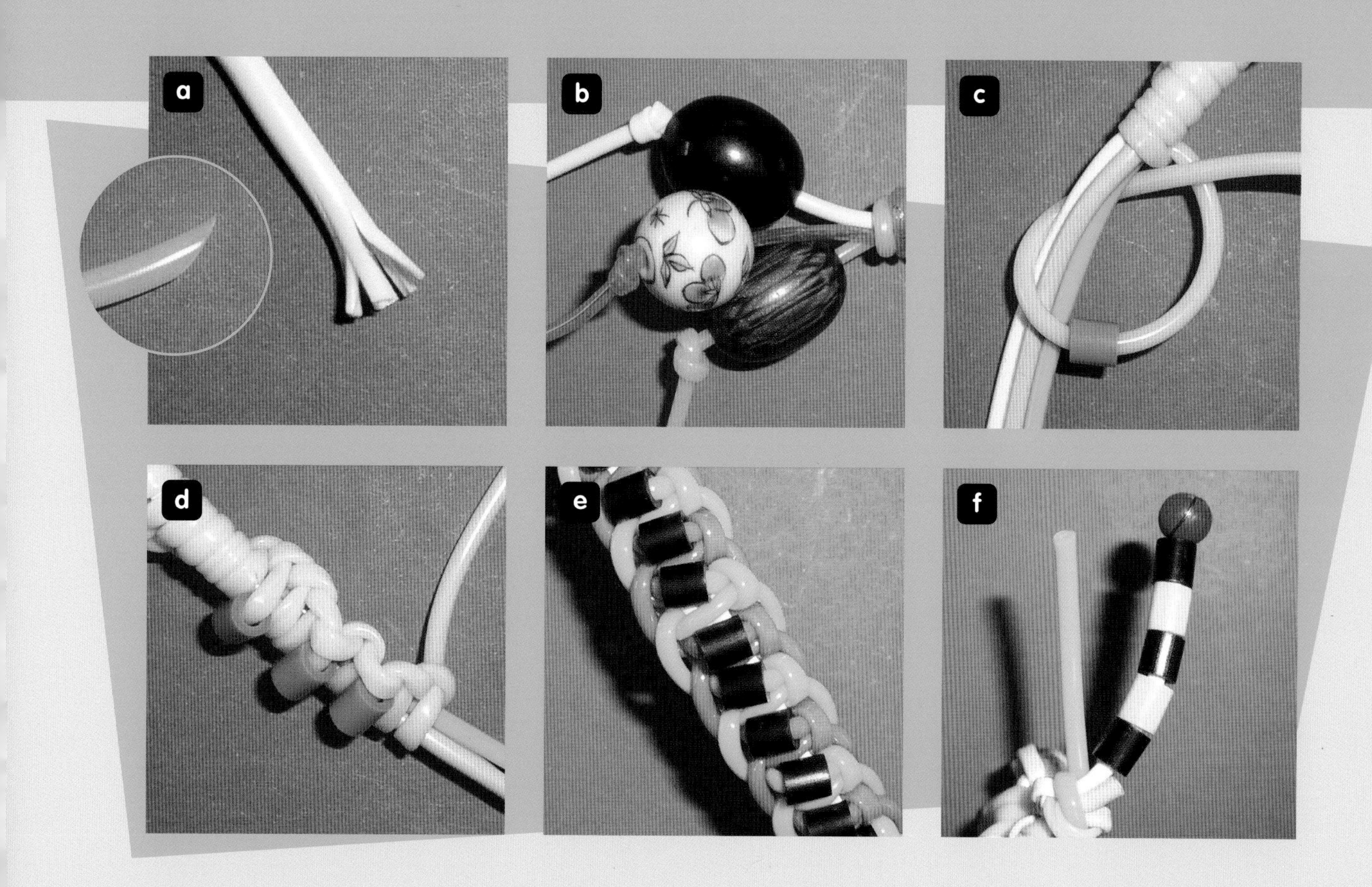
a
b
c
d
e
f

You can create a whole variety of projects with scoubidou strands; you are only limited by your imagination (and the length of your strings!).

Rings and Tags

Rings and tags are good first projects to do, as both of these can easily be woven into simple designs.

Rings

You will need a split ring (you can get these from key cutting shops) to do these projects.

a Take a split ring and make a granny knot around it.

b Now make your **'Off We Go' Stitch** in the normal way and begin your project.

c If you have a project that you have already completed, you can thread the split ring through the **'Off We Go' Stitch**. Getting an adult to help you, open the split pin with a screwdriver and push the strand onto the ring. Do not thread it through your **'Time to Stop' Stitch** as the weight of the keys can pull it undone.

Tags

It is easiest to begin with a ready-made luggage tag to create your project. These often come with suitcases and can also be bought from hardware and key cutting shops.

d When making luggage tags it is important that the scoubidou can't be detached. For this reason, it is a good idea to weave the tag into the middle of your design. Link the tag into the first loop of a stitch.

e When completing the project, choose a simple design that will be not come apart. A simple bead design works well.

f Scoubidous can also be simply tied onto bag handles for easy identification.

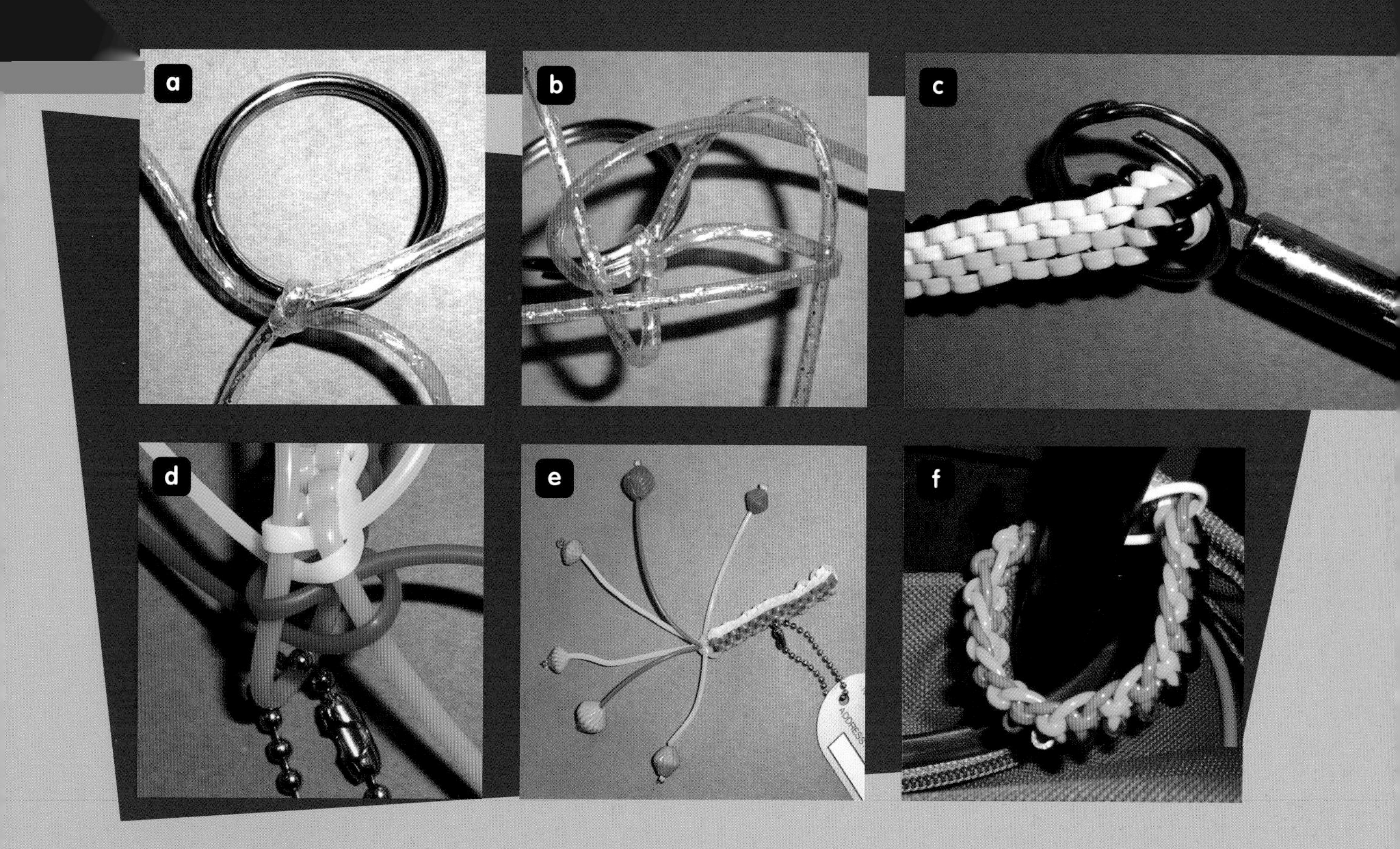
a
b
c
d
e
f
ADDRESS

Bracelets and Bands

These are good second projects to do as they take slightly longer and need carefully fastening together.

Woven Wrap It! Stitch Bracelet

Try wearing two or three of these bracelets in different thicknesses together.

a You will need: two or four scoubidou strands; a tube of plastic or cardboard (such as a piece of washing-up liquid bottle (ask an adult to help you cut this); decoration such as sequins or ribbons.

b Make a granny knot with two scoubidou strands, ready to start a **'Moving On' Wrap it! Stitch**. You can also use four strands and double these up to make a thicker stitch.

Begin your **'Moving On' Wrap It! Stitch**, looping the middle of the stitch around the tube.

c Pull each stitch tightly and push the strands together so that you can't see any of the tube underneath.

Continue with the stitch until the whole tube is covered.

Pull the last stitch through the first stitch so that it doesn't pull apart.

Finish off by securing the strands together in a reef knot inside the tube.

d Decorate your bracelet with ribbons, beads or sequins using thin wire or thread.

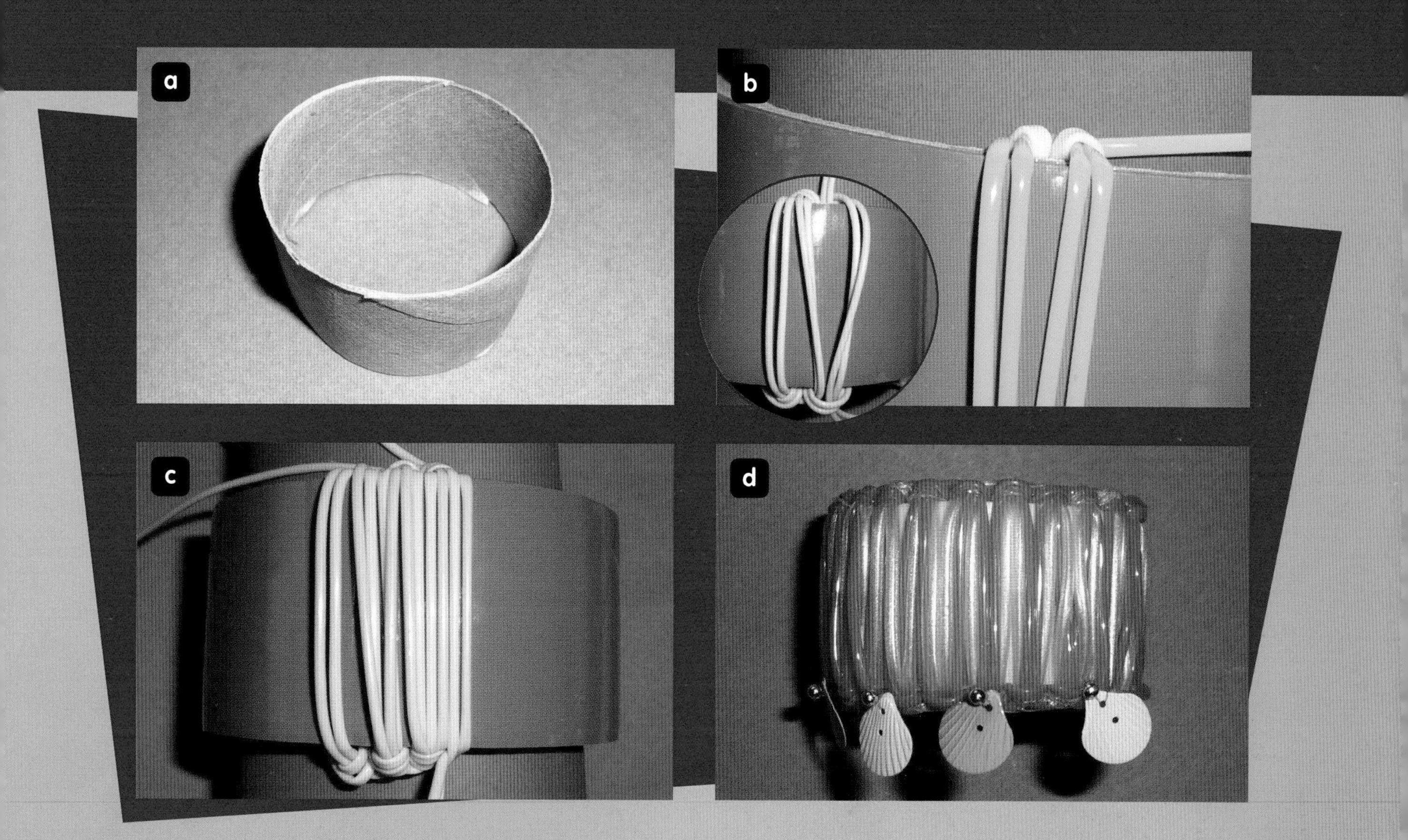
a
b
c
d

Free-style Round & Round Stitch Bracelet

These bracelets are really easy to make and look professional.

a You will need: four scoubidou strands – two of one colour, two of another; a medium gauge jewellery wire; a needle; a fastener for a necklace (we have used a screw fastener).

b Thread the jewellery wire through both strands of the same colour and thread it through the needle about 15cm. Thread this free end back down the same end of the strand.

c Pull the strand from the end you originally started threading to pull the blunt end of the needle back down into strand 2. Pull until the tip of the needle is about 8cm from the end of this strand.

d Carefully push the needle out through the wall of the strand and …

e … thread one part of the fastener on to the end of the wire, securing it with a double knot.

Now thread jewellery wire through both of the other two same colour threads, leaving about 5cm of wire poking out of each end.

Create an **'Off We Go' Box Stitch** at the point where the fastener has come out and the second pair of strands meet in the middle.

Now continue with **'Moving On' Round & Round Stitch** until you have come to about 1cm from the end of the shortest strand.

➤ Continued on page 50

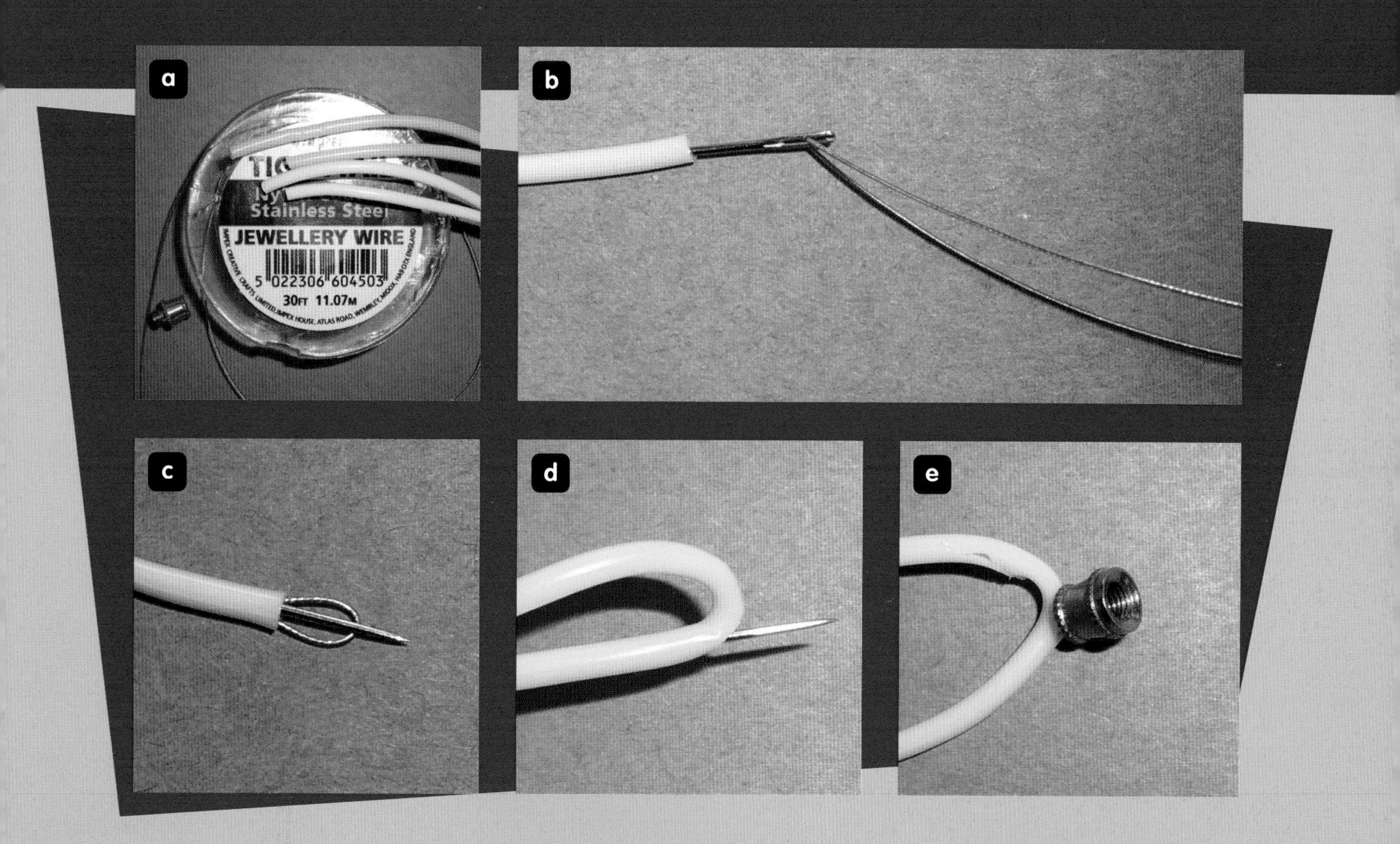
a
Stainless Steel
JEWELLERY WIRE
5 022306 604503
30FT 11.07M
b
c
d
e

➤ **Free-style Round & Round Stitch Bracelet** continued

Thread the second part of the fastener onto the wire on this short strand and secure with a double knot. You will probably have about 0.75cm of raw wire on show.

f Complete three **'Moving On' 1, 2, 3 Stitches** around the bare wire.

g Now do two **'Moving On' Helter Skelter Stitches** with the remaining three strands and …

h … finish off the remaining tassels with beads.

Flower Scrunchy

Scrunchies can be decorated with scoubidou strands by attaching the design at a single point on the scrunchy. This is because the scoubidou won't stretch around the hair if it is secured all the way round.

a This scrunchy design is in the shape of a flower.

You will need: eight scoubidou strands – two of one colour, the rest of another; a medium gauge jewellery wire and a scrunchy.

b Begin by joining strands together with wire to create a double length **Helter Skelter** project. If you use four strands (eight for the double length); three in the centre and one wrapping around them, the flower will be nice and big.

When the project is finished, wrap the **Helter Skelter** around itself twice, as if you are making a big knot, adjusting the spirals to fit into each other.

Secure the ends of the scrunchy with **Wrap It! Stitch**.

c Tie off the loose ends.

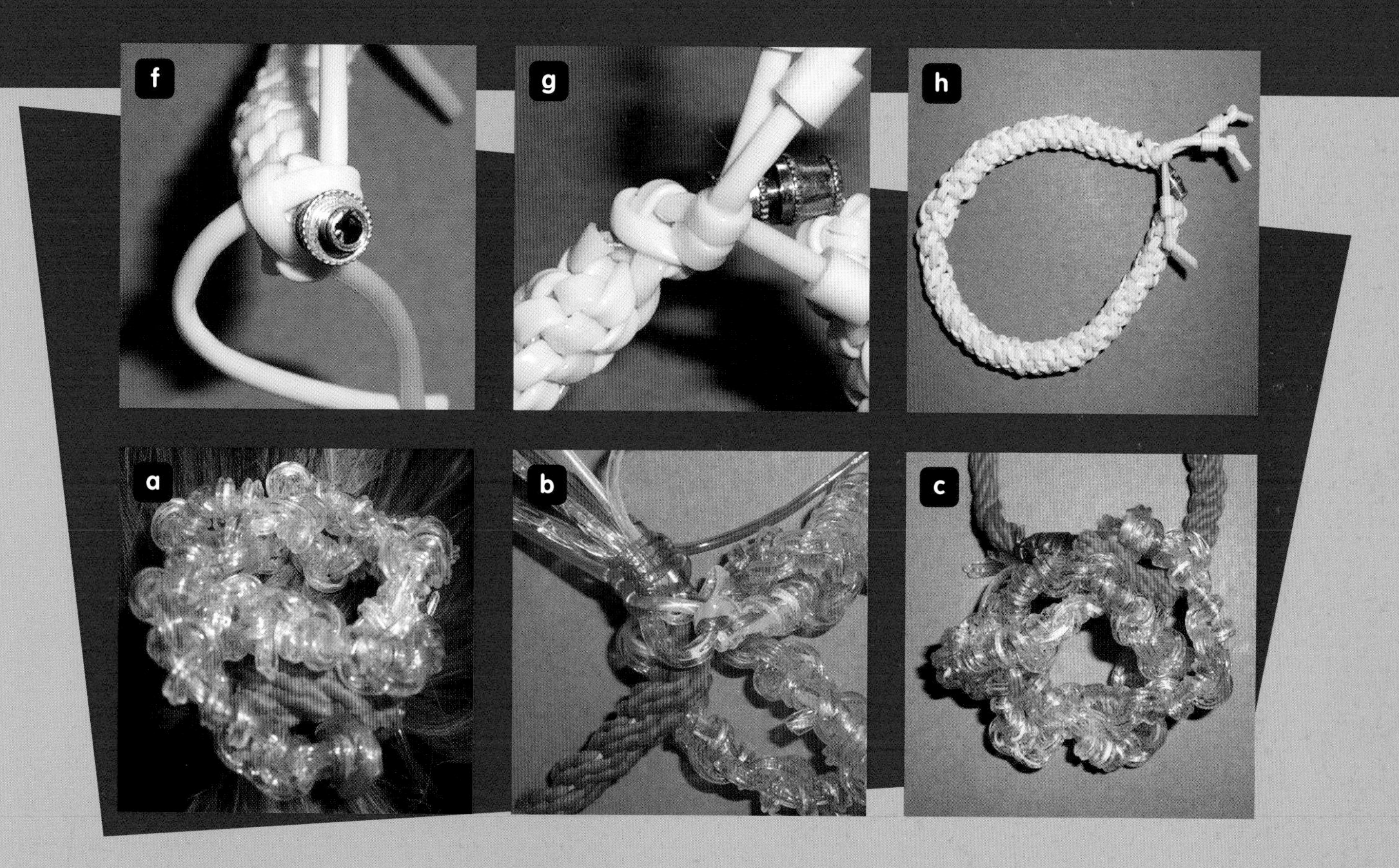
f
g
h
a
b
c

Fairies and Goblins

Fairies, goblins and other fantasy creatures work well if you put wire through their legs and arms before starting. They can also be decorated with material and beads to make them look more realistic.

Felicity Fairy

This fairy design is the basis for the goblin as well. Just add a wired nose and ribbon wings to make the goblin!

You will need: three scoubidou strands – all different colours; a medium gauge jewellery wire; fine gauge jewellery wire (for sewing on eyes and clothes); beads for hands and feet; material for clothes.

- **a** Make the head using **'Moving On' Box Stitch**.
- **b** Now make the arms and legs by using cut-off strands with wire threaded through, secured by beads.
- **c** Secure the arms with a **Box Stitch**.
- **d** Continue with **Wrap it! Stitch** to make the body.

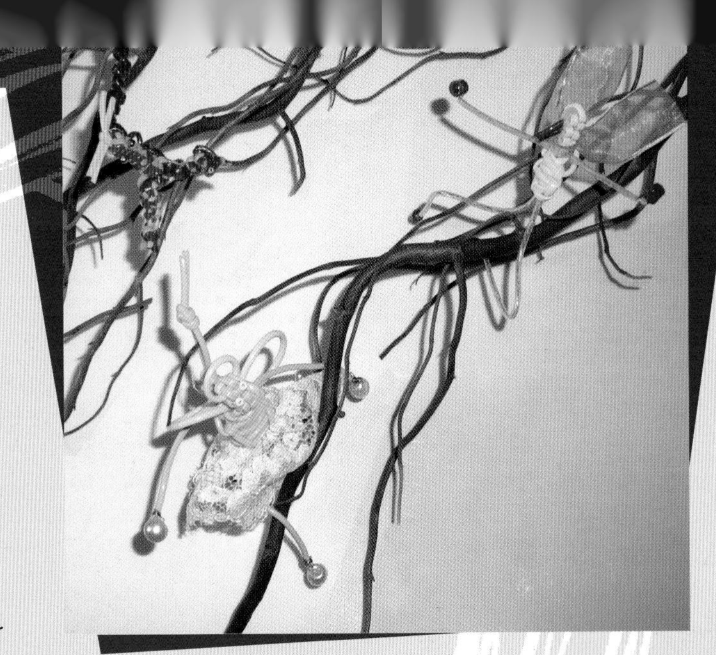

- **e** When the body has reached the required length, add on the legs by looping the **Wrap It! Stitch** under them to 'tie' them in.
- **f** Work back up the body again, using **Wrap It! Stitch** to thicken the tummy up.

➤ Continued on page 54

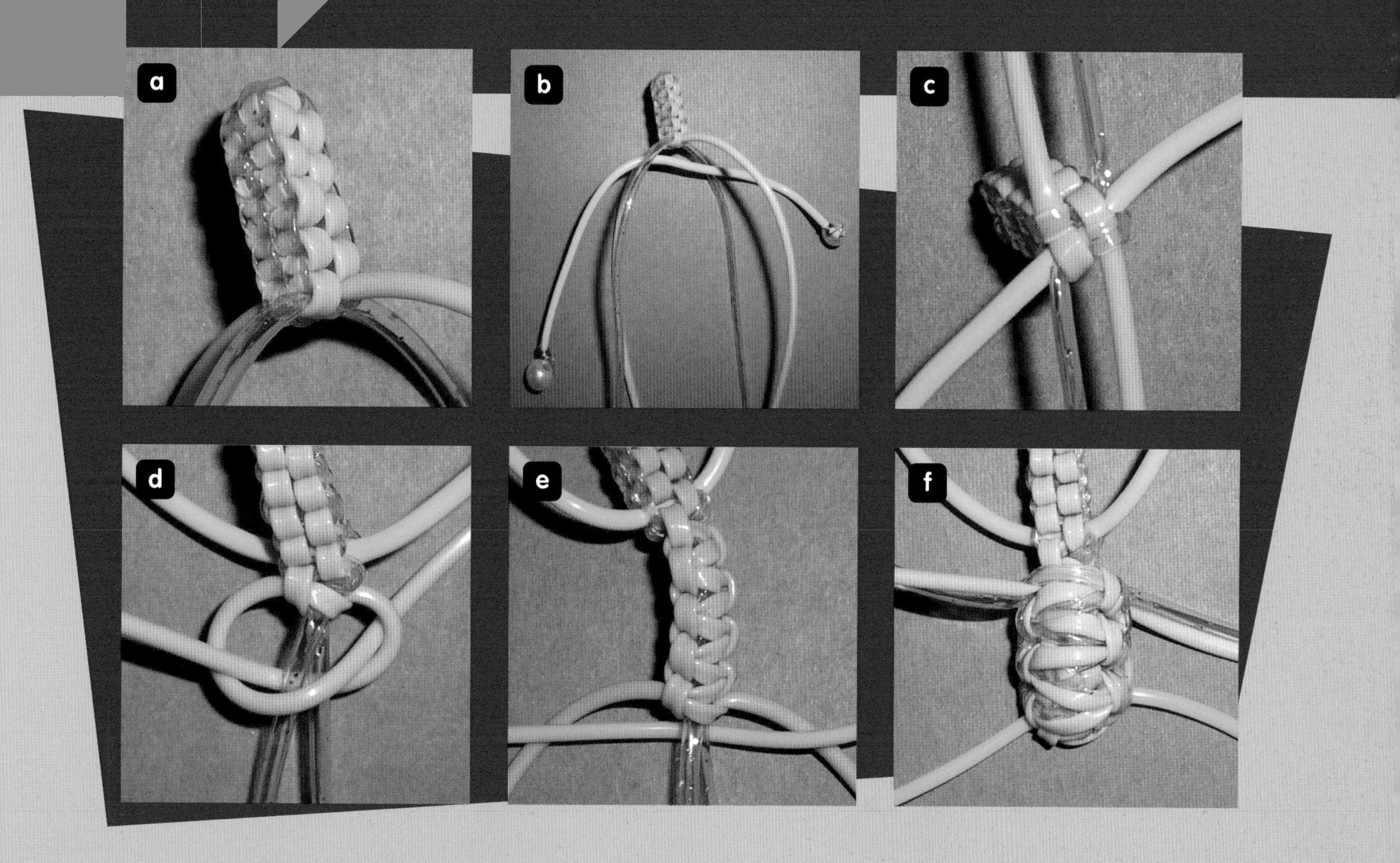
a
b
c
d
e
f

➤ **Fairies and Goblins** continued

g Make a final loose **Wrap It! Stitch** to make the wings, tightening up before the loops are pulled through.

If you don't want to make wings, just secure with a final knot and tie in a granny knot to create a hanging loop.

h Add clothes, eyes and hair to your fairy to make her special!

Under the Sea

Sea creatures make good scoubidou projects as the tassel ends can be made into tentacles. Starfish are simple to do, simply by joining **Box Stitch** sections, as explained in 'Triple joins' on page 34 (see picture **a** opposite).

Otis Octopus

Pass wire through the strands before you begin if you want the octopus to have bendy legs.

You will need: six scoubidou strands; fine gauge jewellery wire or cotton (for sewing on eyes); four beads for the eyes; twelve beads for the legs.

b Leave 7cm free at the end of the strands and then tie a granny knot.

Continue with **'Moving On' Do the Twist! Stitch** until you can bend your octopus round in a circle, like Otis Octopus in the picture.

Pull both ends together, undo the granny knot and do **'Moving On' Helter Skelter Stitch** to pull the ends tight. Choose eight strands for legs and cut the others close to the last stitch. Decorate the feet with beads and wire on the eyes.

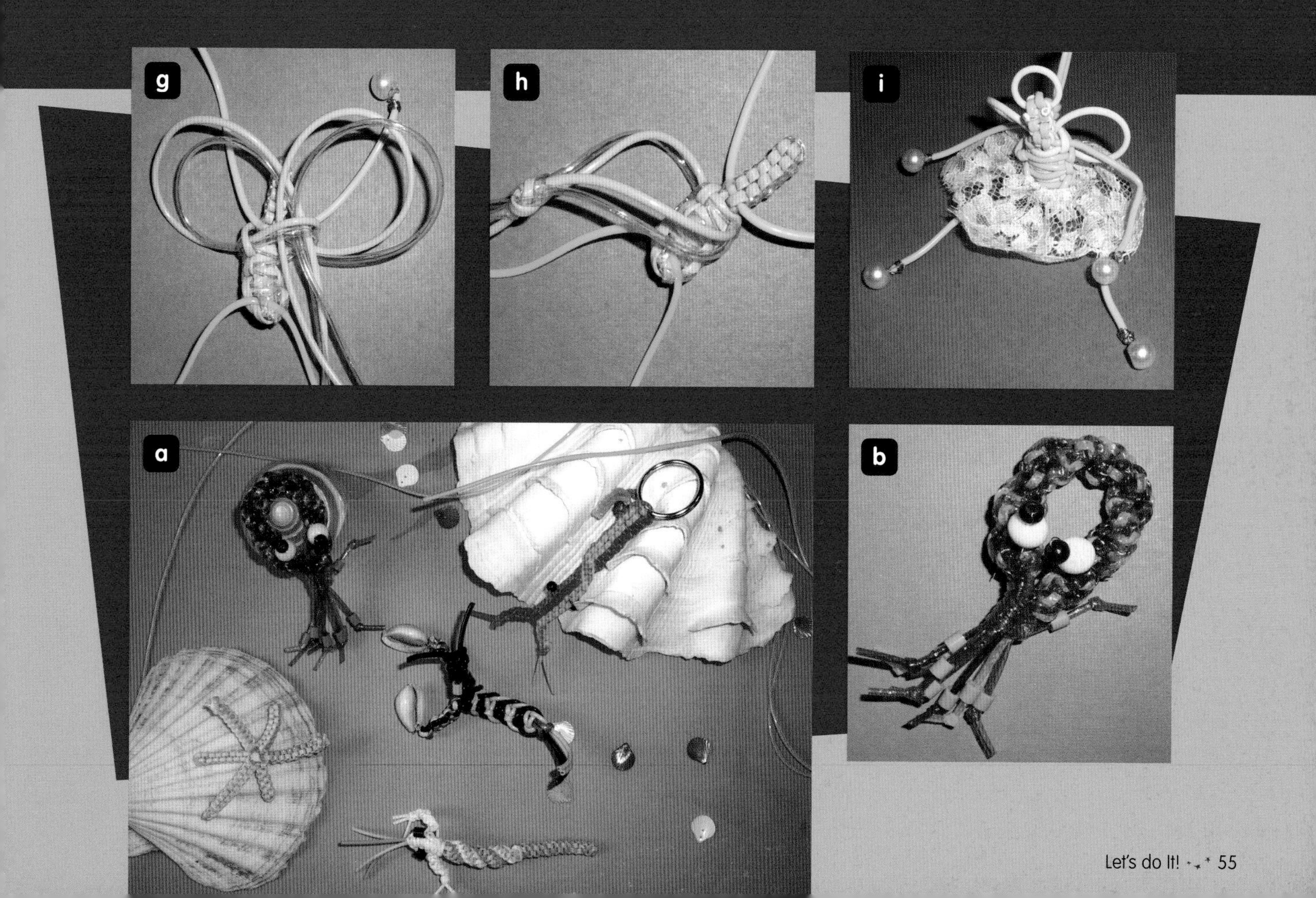
g
h
i
a
b

Let's do It!

➤ **Under the Sea** continued

Sally Shrimp

This shrimp works well as a key-ring although you can leave the ring out if you prefer.

You will need: three scoubidou strands – two of one colour, one of another; a split ring; fine gauge jewellery wire or cotton (for sewing on eyes); two beads for the eyes.

a Begin by tying a split ring into your project using **'Off We Go' Over & Under Stitch**.

b Complete about twelve **'Moving On' Over & Under Stitches**.

c Now continue using **'Moving On' Do the Twist! Stitch** for three more stitches.

Now go back to **'Moving On' Over & Under Stitch** for another twelve stitches.

d Thread beads onto the odd colour strands to make eyes (or secure fine beads with jewellery wire).

e Fasten the eyes in with the next stitch.

f Now complete six more **'Moving On' Over & Under Stitches**.

Split the strands into two sets of three.

Complete six **'Moving On' 1, 2, 3 Stitches** with each set of strands.

Finally, create a **'Time to Stop' 1, 2, 3 Stitch** to finish off each end. Trim the ends to make feelers.

Your shrimp is now complete!

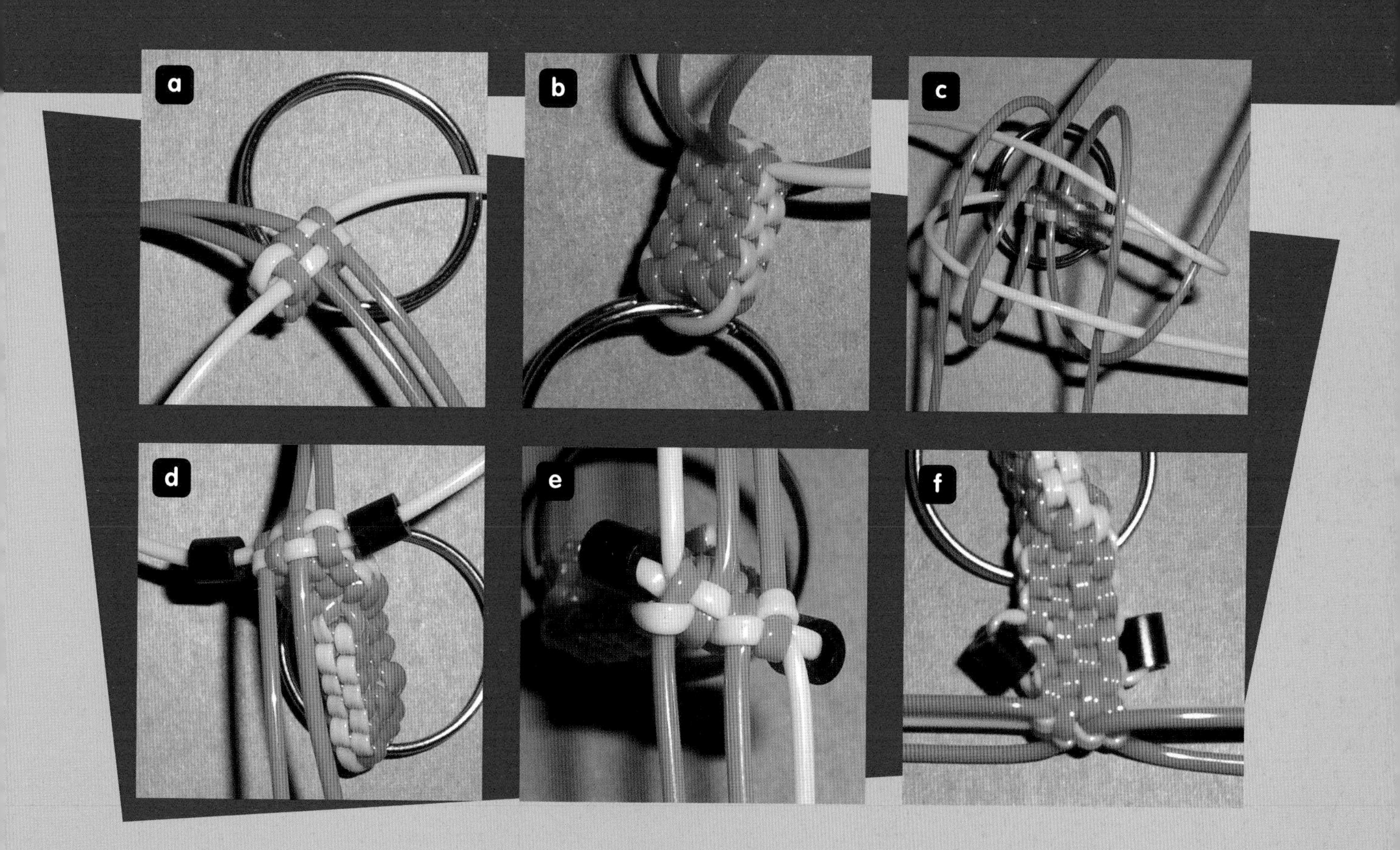
a
b
c
d
e
f

Lenny Lobster

Lobsters look great if you can find something to use to make their claws. Try making claws out of two strings of beads, knotting together the ends of the strands if you can't find shells. Thread wire through the strands before beginning your lobster.

You will need: five scoubidou strands; medium gauge jewellery wire to thread through the strands; fine gauge jewellery wire or cotton (for sewing on eyes); two beads for the eyes; shells for the claws.

a Make an **'Off We Go' Wrap It! Stitch**, and then continue with **'Moving On' Wrap It! Stitch** to create the body of the lobster (about ten stitches).

b Thread four strands through the last stitch. You will use this later to make the head.

c Now split the original strands into two sets (one of each colour).

d Create the claw arms with seven **'Moving On' 1, 2, 3 Stitches**. Finish the claws off with **'Time to Stop' 1, 2, 3 Stitch**.

Cut the ends off two of the strands on each claw close to the last stitch. Thread the remaining strand onto the shell.

e Create four **'Moving On' Box Stitches** with the strands you attached for the head.

Thread on the eyes and continue for another eight stitches.

Create four **'Moving On' Box Stitches** with the strands you attached for the head and tie the ends as antennae. Snip off the ends.

f Finally, trim the strands at the other end and bend to create the tail.

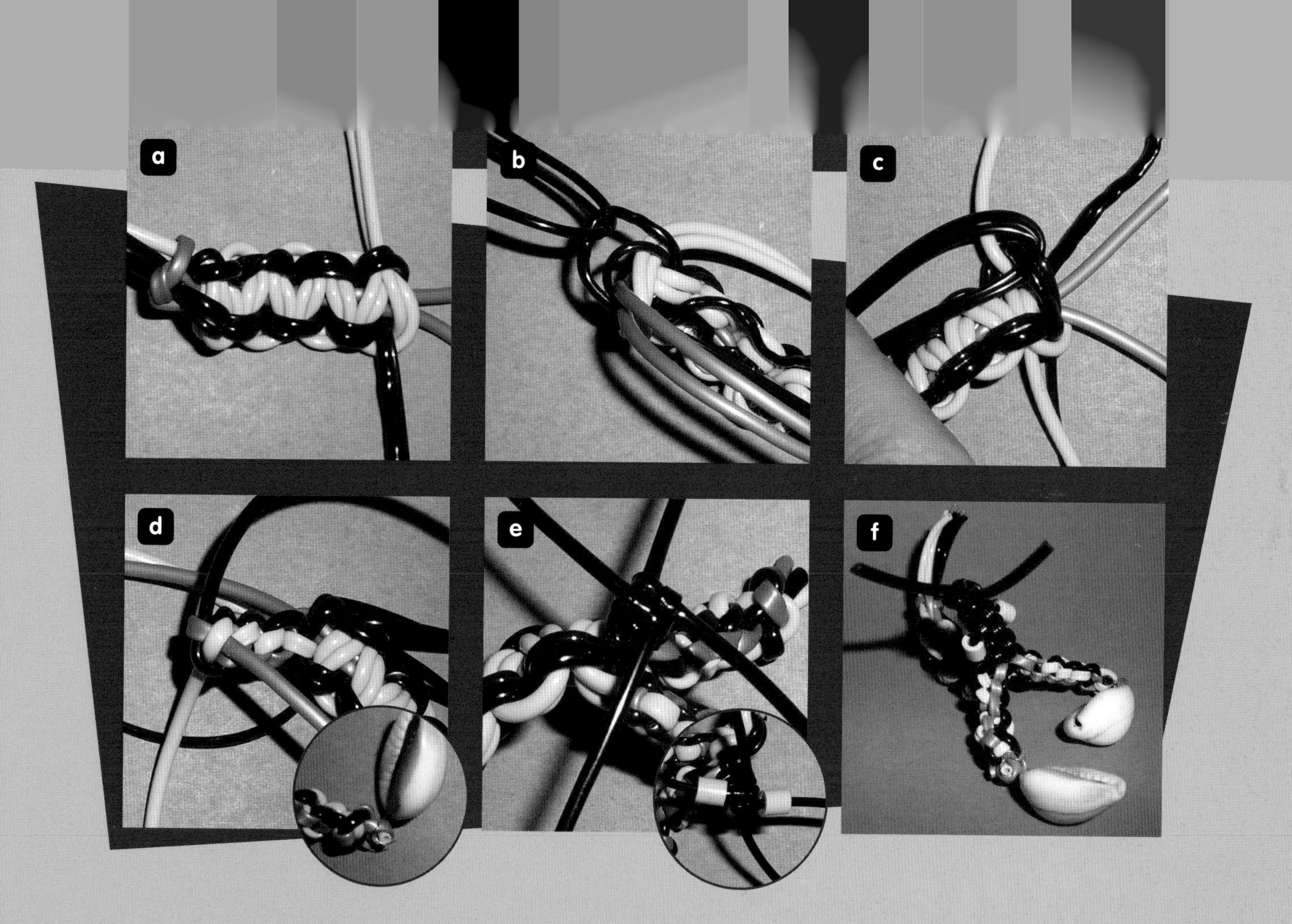
a
b
c
d
e
f

Let's do It!

Creepy Crawlies

Spiders and snakes are great fun to make with wire as you can bend them into different positions when they are completed. Adding beads and bells makes them more realistic (and scary!).

Rapping Rattler

This funky rattlesnake has a bell on its tail to give him rhythm! You can also put him on a key-ring so your keys are easy to find. Thread wire through the strands before you begin if you want your snake to be bendy.

You will need: two scoubidou strands of one colour and two different-coloured strands; two red beads for the eyes; ten beads for the tail; fine gauge jewellery wire or cotton (for sewing on eyes); medium gauge jewellery wire to thread through the body (optional); bell for the rattle.

a Put the same-colour threads together and tie a granny knot with the other two strands about 7cm from the top.

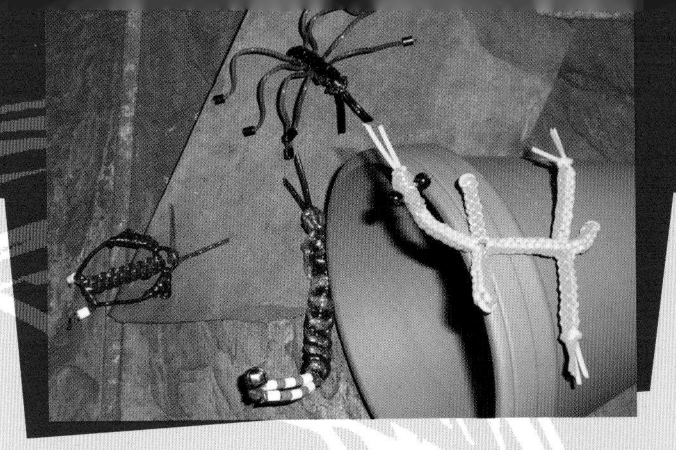

Continue by doing **'Moving On' Caterpillar Stitch** to create the body of the snake (32 individual stitches).

b Now take the two same-coloured centre strands to the outside (blue in this picture) and use these to do the **'Moving On' Caterpillar Stitch** four times.

c Next, thread red beads on to make the eyes.

d Push the strand ends through to the other side of the snake (try using a blunt pencil to help you do this), and tie a knot at the end of each to stop the strands from pulling through. Snip these ends off close to the snake.

e Snip off the ends of two threads of one colour to leave two strands poking out to make the tongue.

f To make the tail, thread beads onto the strands at the other end of the snake and knot them together. Wire the bell to the tail.

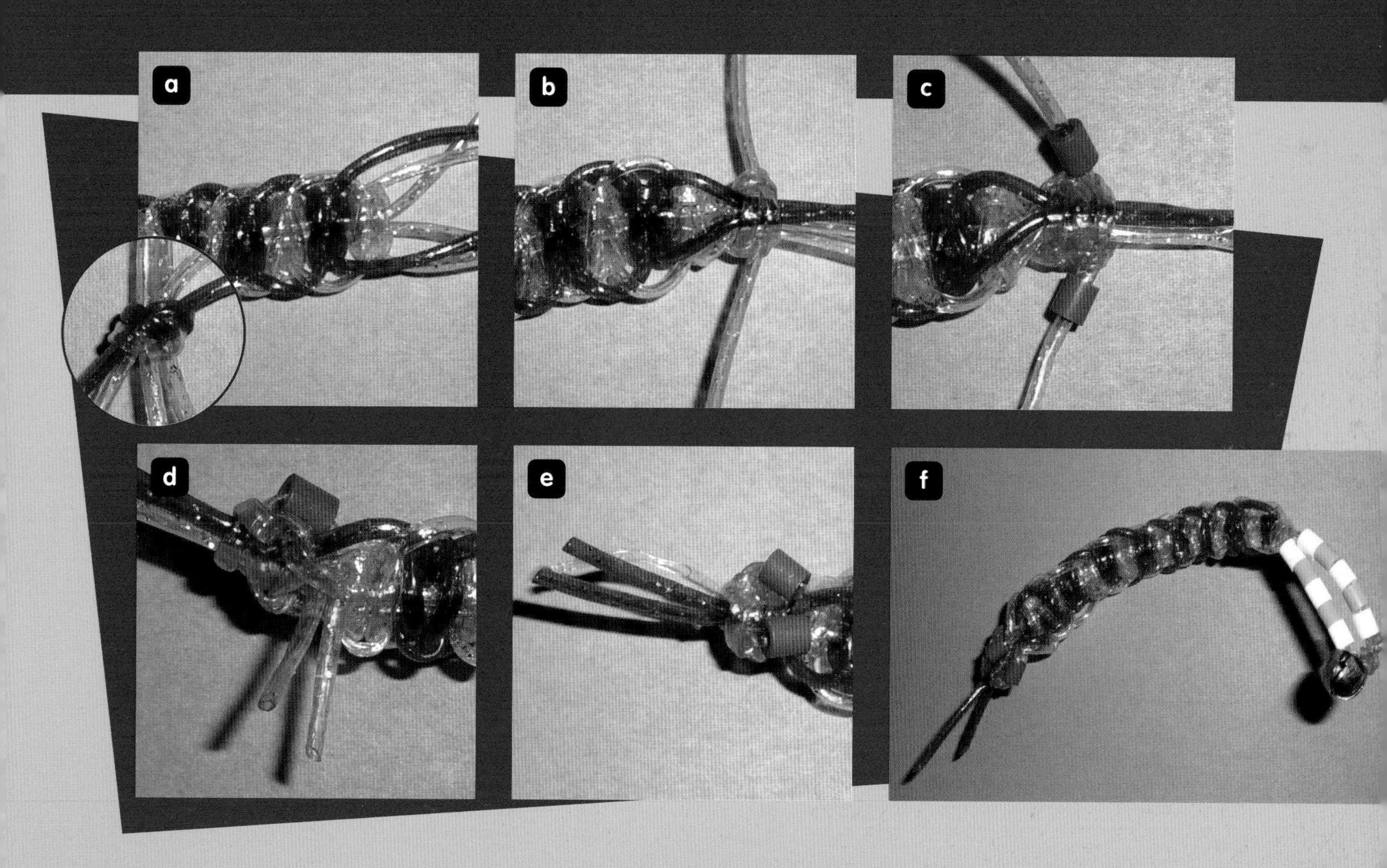
a
b
c
d
e
f

The Lounge Lizard

This cool lizard can also be wired so that he bends wherever you want him to. Remember to wire all the strands you use.

You will need: six scoubidou strands; fine gauge jewellery wire or cotton (for sewing on eyes); two beads for the eyes.

a Create three sections using **'Off We Go' Box Stitch** and **'Moving On' Box Stitch** like this. These form parts 1, 2 and 3 in photograph **f** opposite.

b Take sections 1 and 2 and create a right-angle double join (see page 34).

c Continue with **'Moving On' Box Stitch** down these new sections (one creates the head; one creates the body).

Take section 3 and create another right-angle double join with the body to create the two back legs. Finish these with a **'Time to Stop' Box Stitch** and trim the ends.

d After creating fifteen **'Moving On' Box Stitches** in the head section, continue with one **'Moving On' Wrap It! Stitch**.

e Now work backwards covering the **'Moving On' Box Stitch** for two stitches. Thread on the eyes and continue for another three stitches. Finally, finish with a **'Moving On' Helter Skelter Stitch**, pulling very tight and tie off with a knot.

f Your lizard is complete!

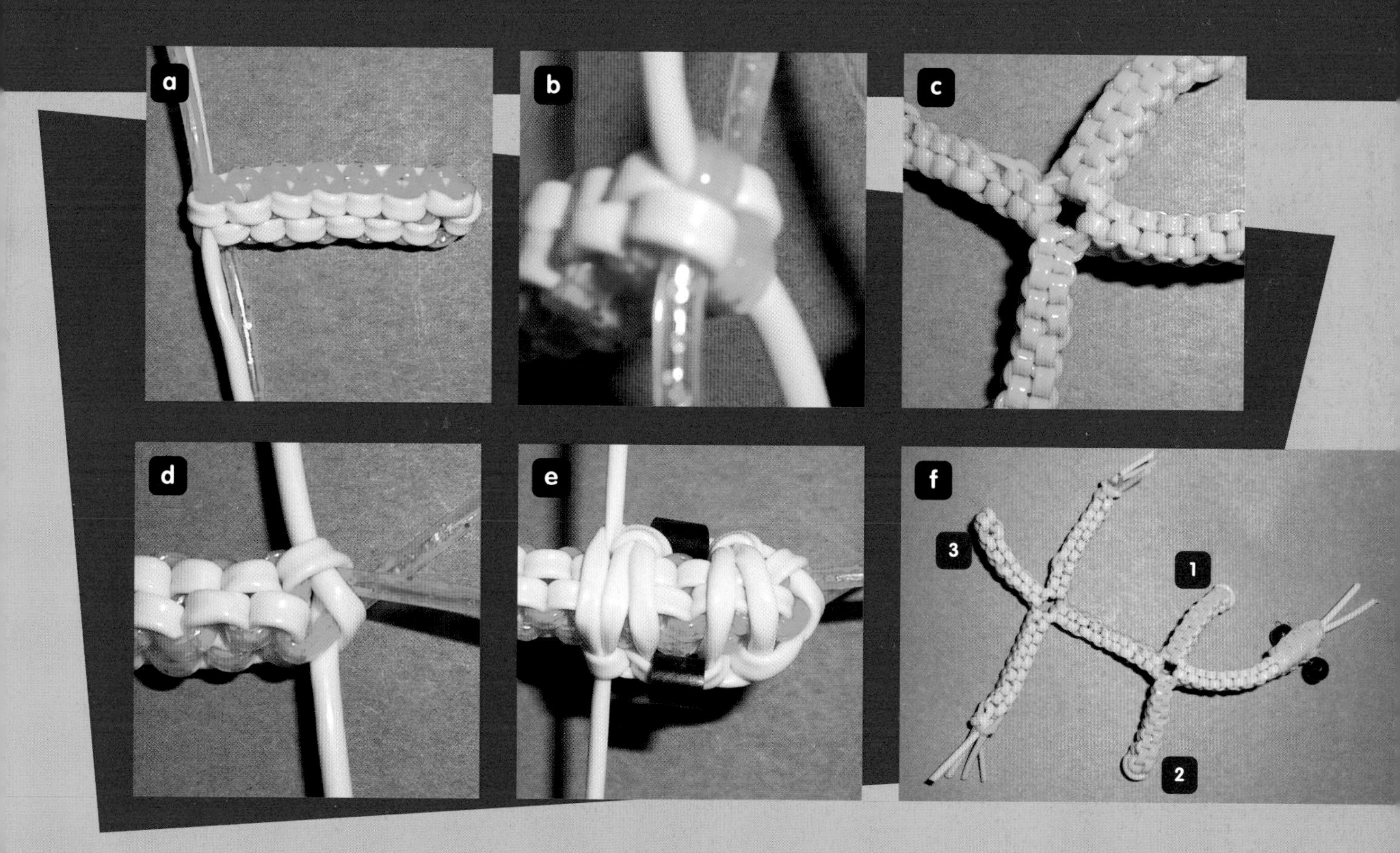
a
b
c
d
e
f
3
1
2

Invent your Own

Now you have been through all the techniques in this book, you will be able to create your own unique projects.

Try adapting stitches to add more strands. We have used **Wrap It! Stitch**, using extra strands and alternating stitches to make this owl just the right size. The broomstick is made with **Round & Round Stitch**.

Sometimes it is good to come up with a theme, such as: Horses and Ponies; Space Rockets; Ghouls and Ghosts. Why not have a competition with your friends to see who can come up with the best project?

You might even be able to persuade your teacher to let you use your scoubidous as an instruction project in class. You never know, they may end up scoubidouing with you, too!